Something Different

Corrine Taig

Acknowledgments

I want to thank Heather Matthews for her wonderful job editing this book. Matt Sabolek for the amazing cover art. Lorana Hoopes for her advice and wisdom on self publishing. I must thank the many beta readers and input givers along the way whom are too many to name. And of course Garrett Taiji for his support, technical help and suggestions throughout the process as well as the lovely flower art. Thanks, Babe!

Contents

Something Different

Corrine Taiji

This book is dedicated to all the amazing women out there working hard every day to show the world what we can do. We make magic.

Chapter 1- It Begins

She stepped out of the golden pond. Drips of sparkling water shone like jewels on her skin. The smells of fresh morning dew and tangy lush plants greeted her senses as she adjusted to land once again. The waiting animal hide caressed her bare skin like a gentle hand as she wrapped it around her. A quick shiver spiraled through her slender body. Suddenly, the snap of a branch — her long red hair swings out behind as she turned toward the sound, her chin thrusting up and eyes enlarging to display their brilliant blue.

"My Queen!" she heard before she could see anything, and then a male bearing official royal messenger crests stepped out of the shrubbery. He paused upon making eye contact then quickly looked down, careful not to show any reaction to her near-naked state.

"You may speak." Her voice was deep, yet richly feminine and gentle, bringing to mind velvet and decadent sweets. "My Queen, a well-trusted spy has returned from your sister's lands with news. Unpleasant news I'm afraid, My Queen."

"I see." Stepping away from the messenger so as to hide her frown, she entered the tent set up for her to dress. Emerging moments later in a robe of thickly woven purple fabric with a soft white fur trim, she tried to smile. She extended her delicate pale hand toward him, her opal-like nails gleaming in the sun's rays.

"You may continue."

"My Queen, the spy informs us that your sister, Princess Alara, has started to amass armies and that she has plans to invade. The reports say that she has befriended others … not … not entirely human." The messenger looks pained, briefly looking up at the Queen's face before turning his eyes down, clenching his hands behind his back.

Realizing her mouth was hanging open and eyes were bulging, she made great effort to return to her normal calm expression. "Thank you for bringing me the news, good sir. I know it is not easy to bear information others may not want to hear. Please see my guard behind the hut. She will reward you for your service."

"Yes, My Queen."

Emmeldine once again entered her tent and wrote a quick message on her royal stationary, then lit a flame in a clear dish and burned the remaining parchment to ash. She alerted her guards, and they all headed back to the castle.

After bathing and dressing in more properly royal attire, Emmeldine sat down in her chambers, fingering the beaded chain in her hand. The smooth wood orbs felt warm in her fingers as she gently placed it back on her chest. She took several long, deep breaths, looked around to make sure no one had entered unannounced, and finally allowed a few swollen tears to leak down her alabaster cheeks. The pain of her sister's hatred was not unknown to her, but despite their sordid history, this development still took her aback. That she would take things to this degree was quite surprising. Surprising and possibly disastrous in so many ways. Emmeldine wrung her hands and trembled, contemplating bringing in forces she had never dreamed of when she was crowned Queen a mere six years ago. Could she fight her own sister?

With a heavy heart, she rang a bell and a young serving lad entered.

"Yes, my Queen?" The pale boy bowed.

"Please summon my Priestess immediately. Tell her to come to my waiting room with great haste."

"Yes, My Queen."

She walked slowly to the chamber, knowing it would take longer for the Priestess to arrive and dreading the task before her. Emmeldine, Queen in her own castle, royal born and bred, reached out a shaking hand to turn the knob before her. Inside her waiting room she saw the box, laid out on her table as requested. The box was a dark wood from ancient times, engraved with gold, luminous in its splendor. It was alluring and daunting all at once. The chamber was empty of all maids and ladies; she was alone. Sitting down on the stool beside the box, she waited. Allowing one last tear as approaching footsteps neared, she hurriedly wiped it away before the Priestess cleared the threshold. Green eyes squinted in questioning concern and blue eyes shone back in determination mixed with fear. One nod of the Queen's head and the Priestess slid forward, her large, soft body filling the space between them. She picked up the box, stared intently at the Queen, and began a soft, melodic chant. The Queen's voice joined her, at first with a waver then soon gaining intensity. The two women's voices rose in volume and power until the entire room rang with palpable energy.

Suddenly the box flew from the Priestess' hands and landed on the floor with a thud. The women's eyes widened as they saw it start to glow. The ethereal light, in colors they had no words for, overtook the entire structure and the box opened slowly. One tiny wing peeked out, then another. A shimmering little creature zipped straight toward the Queen, landing lightly on the table in front of her.

Emmeldine stared at the creature in heavy silence. Its otherworldly eyes, smaller than the end of her quill looked up at her expectantly, piercing into her soul. Tiny rainbow-hued wings beat as fast as a startled bird's, yet did not appear to change position in the air. Magic. Her spirit lightened upon seeing the beautiful little sprite. *Perhaps it wouldn't be so bad. This wouldn't have to equal certain doom; perhaps things could be different.* Still, it was with a heavy heart that she gave her command, and the little creature, a miracle in itself, zoomed off to another realm not even the Queen could visit, a place no Priestess had actually seen, to gather the forces necessary to protect Emmeldine's home.

The Queen's gaze followed the Priestess as she picked up the ancient relic and placed it gingerly back on its shelf. Her eyes fixed on the closed lid. She heard a faint drip from the windowpane, the soft shuffle of feet in the hall, and the pounding of her own heart. A rich smell of roasted meats and savory dishes filled the room, but she didn't notice. The cold stones pulsed under her feet and a shiver passed through her body like the breath of a curse. Her eyes fluttered shut and instantly reopened, fixing on the box. She waited.

Chapter 2 - What Was Then

Back before certain stars had aligned and suns had forever set, there were two little girls. They knew nothing of magic or mystical things, yet their lives were filled with them. One fair with hair of red and eyes the turquoise of happy dreams. The other a darker hue as if her skin were kissed by the cosmos itself and turned a golden bronze. Her eyes were the green of emeralds and her hair a golden wave of thick silk. These girls played together and shared the same mother but had different fathers, a common occurrence in royal families of the lands.

The red-haired girl, Emmeldine, was fathered by Reynaldo, the proper King of Trimeria: ordained in marriage by the High Priestess herself, blessed by the Goddess. Reynaldo had been chosen as the Queen's mate for his handsome features and good breeding, as was also common for this land ruled by women. He had been raised by a prominent family of weavers who had curiously uncommon success in whatever they pursued, and his mother had been very close to the former Queen. Rumors of magic had flared up from time to time surrounding his family's estates but had been put out briskly like the candles that lit their rooms at bedtime. Reynaldo had a thin face with highly-structured features, large, clear blue eyes with hidden depths, and a tall muscular body thought good for reproduction. His hair was red.

Alara had been fathered by the Queen's lover, Dono. Dono was shorter and less refined, but found very attractive by the court ladies. He was a Warrior — muscular with dark, heavy features that appeared romantic late at night. At least the Queen thought so. As a Warrior, Dono was often gone from the palace. This pleased Reynaldo but left Queen Maraleine lonely for male companionship. Her eyes wandered.

It was during one of these absences that we find young princess Emmeldine and younger princess Alara in the courtyard, searching for Fairy flowers.

"Alara! Slow down, Alara! Why must you always run so? I want to find the Fairies!"

"My Dono says there are no such things as Fairies! He says it's common and beneath me to think of such things."

"Oh? And I suppose running around like a fool, jumping and trotting like a wild mare is respectable, is it?" Emmeldine chided, but had a big smile on her face — her eyes sparkling with affection. She patted Alara on the head and pulled her into her lap, sitting back on the dry brown grass. "Little sister, it is time I tell you of the wonders of our realm. Of magic beasts and flying things, of fairies and phantoms, of love and hate." Emmeldine squinted and her lips pursed as she waved her hands up above her head.

Eyes wide, Alara stopped squirming and looked up at her big sister, twisting in her lap to see her face more clearly. "But, my Dono..."

"For goodness sake Alara, he's your father, not your Dono! His *name* is Dono. My father's name is Reynaldo but I call him Father, or King Father in public. You may call yours Father, or Papa, or Warrior Dono around others." Emmeldine smiled down at her little sister, shaking her head gently.

Alara remained quiet and her smile faded, as did the sparkle in her eyes — but she listened. Emmeldine went on to talk about tales of yore. Stories told in ale houses and kitchens alike, even those on castle grounds into which young children might find their way. Stories about Fairies, Crowlers, Mikles, Cats and Bats with special powers, Ogres and more. Tale after tale she told until she realized Alara had fallen asleep in her lap. Tenderly, Emmeldine pulled up the cloak to cover her sister's small body, then waved for her minder to carry Alara back to her chambers. She followed to see her gently put to bed, then kissed her cheek on the way out.

The next day, Emmeldine and Alara were playing in their wing of the castle. The vast, bleak chambers of stone rang vacantly with their gleeful laughter. The children's wing was meant to hold a nursery full of babies, seeming to mock the Queen, who had not conceived in some years. Reynaldo was eyed with distrust.

Emmeldine was chasing Alara around pretending to be an Ogre, and Alara was screaming playfully, her blond braids bouncing bountifully. Emmeldine's hair was up in a mature weave of complex braids that ringed her petite skull like a fiery red halo. She had started her royal training earlier that season and was taking a break to burn off some of her youthful energy, too young yet to be confined to the classroom all day.

"Alara! Wait, slow down, you can't go in there!" Emmeldine followed her little sister into a waiting room adjacent to their mother's chambers. She quietly rushed to Alara's side, not wanting to alert anyone of their presence lest they be scolded. She went to grab Alara's hand, intending to pull her out of the empty room, but paused when she heard an unfamiliar voice.

"*Dom ra leh bah. Ne mo frum.*" She did not recognize the language, but felt a tingle shoot up from the root of her spine and dissipate through her skull. Her nose tickled. Then suddenly, a voice she did recognize, loud and strong: her mother.

"Shaima, please, use more! This has to work, I can't afford *not* to conceive. You heard the prophecy. Too much is at stake." Emmeldine had never heard this tone in her mother's voice before. She sounded shrill, lacking the confidence she was known for. Queen Maraleine never wavered.

Silence. Then, more low, murmured chanting. Suddenly, a flash of crimson light radiated out from under the chamber door. The tingling returned to Emmeldine's spine and face, her hand instinctively rising to her cheek to rub it tentatively. Glancing down, she saw Alara rub her own cheek and her eyes enlarge like a spectre's. Her face was as white as marble. Her body slowly softening, Emmeldine tried to relax. She squeezed Alara's hand gently, leading her back the way they had come, treading softly on the cold grey stone.

When they entered the nursery, Alara went straight to her wood doll and started to run her fingers up and down the length of its corn silk hair, eyes downcast and lips tight. Emmeldine thought to distract her while covering up her own confusion.

With a tight smile, she cleared her throat and chose a light tone: "I learned the most interesting thing in my lessons this morn. It was about measurement, how we know the distance between things or how we speak of it."

Alara's eyes stayed down and she was as quiet as a mouse.

Emmeldine pressed on, "We speak of short distances by strands, as you've heard. Well, when we say someone is five strands tall, that means five strands of beads. But not just any beads, Alara. Do you know whose beads the entire realm measures by?"

A soft whisper, "No."

"Our mother's! The entire realm measures distances by our mother's wooden strand of beads. They are the basic unit of measurement for all of Trimeria!"

Alara looked up, her wide eyes blinking. "Really? Mother's beads that she always wears?"

"Yes! Isn't that remarkable? Our mother is the highest ruler, of course — yet I had no idea the beads passed down from our grandmother's line held such importance."

"The beads will one day be yours? All of Trimeria will belong to you?" Alara's face tightened again as she looked back down at her doll's yellow hair.

"Well — yes, I suppose... in a manner of speaking. But

dear sister, I certainly hope you will help me rule; I hope you will be by my side." Emmeldine smiled brightly at her sister's downturned head, then jumped up upon seeing her language teacher approach. "I must go back to my training. Fare thee well — I will dine with you later." Emmeldine bounced off down the long hall, not looking back at her sister... who had silently begun to cry.

Chapter 3- What Happens Next (Now)

The weight of her own body as she forced herself through her chamber doors was like a giant stone. Heavily taking one step after another, she barely heard the soft scrape of the well-trained guards as they followed. Eyes darted to the dull grey wall outside her private domain, a flutter in her belly when she remembered the dampening charm her Priestess Shaima had put there only recently. *Had they been heard?*

Emmeldine thought back to the first extensive meeting she had with her Priestess about magic, before possible battle was on either of their minds.

"My Queen, I do believe the people are ready to know more. There is magic all around them yet they are blind. Might we open their eyes?"

"They know. They know if they choose to listen. Are not the tales told and stories recounted, passed down from family to family by mother and father alike? They don't want it to be true. From what I understand, embracing magic was nearly the end of womankind. Do we dare even think of risking that again?"

"I feel we must. There are leaks. Magic flows and bends around all. It is only a matter of time." The Priestess met the Queen's eyes and opened her hands before her, pinkies touching, as was the proper way to show respect to the ordained ruler. Her pale brown hair, almost golden, was streaked with grey, falling into her face. She gently pushed it behind her ear, showing a wrinkled neck and cheek. The Queen eyed her thoughtfully.

"Shaima, it is true you have served my family well for many rotations of the planets. My mother was very fond of you, which is why I kept you on. But please know this: when it comes to magic, I am no fool. I have learned from history, from the past. Great Queens before me have died from it, cities have fallen, oceans run dry. I know there is beauty and healing within magic itself, and of course I wish we could access that light, but at what cost?" Her flawless porcelain brow wrinkled and her eyes tightened as she looked away. She clasped the beads around her neck and fingered them. The Priestess opened her mouth to protest, and Emmeldine thrust a hand up toward her. "Please, let's not speak of this again."

The council chamber was large and cold and its stone walls blank, except for a few random tapestries showing scenes of benevolent Queens bestowing gifts upon the people. A low murmur of conversation suddenly stopped. Emmeldine's cheeks flamed as she realized her right hand was clenched tightly around her left and she was biting her bottom lip. All eyes were on her.

Emmeldine cleared her throat and relaxed her body. As her mouth began to open, a soft yet determined voice spoke first.

"The spies report discontent in the villages. Some of the townsfolk are worried you won't choose a mate. They fear there will be no female offspring to secure the throne."

Emmeldine waved her hand dismissively at her childhood playmate. "What else, Daria? Surely there is more for you to be so anxious? I know you're not that concerned about my romantic life!" "I fear you know me well, Your Majesty. I see our years of sharing your nursery have made it impossible for me to hide my feelings from you. As it should be." A shallow bow as she grinned broadly, eyes twinkling. "Grumblings have been heard about odd happenings in the woods and the possibility of evil beings encroaching. I'm sure it's all silly nonsense... but fear spreads rapidly, My Queen."

Emmeldine squinted. She realized she was frowning and forced a smile. Looking aside, she caught Shaima's eye. Shaima offered a weak smile with a slight head bob and swiftly looked away.

Emmeldine felt Daria's stare directed at her and turned back toward her sharply. Daria's eyes widened and she talked rapidly to fill the silence.

"Mostly though, the farmers, shopkeepers and tradesfolk keep on as they always have — passing down knowledge from mother to daughter, and these days, even from father to son. More and more males have been able to control their aggression and prove themselves, and thus are being allowed out into the fields and shops."

Emmeldine's heart filled with warmth upon hearing this. Her neutral expression cracked with the power of her radiant smile, her eyes twinkling. She gestured around the room, "I am ever so pleased Daria, my dear friend, to see that you and several others on the council have brought male assistants here today. I do encourage this. As you know, I have commissioned a group to look into how to best integrate males more into palace life, and I am eager to hear their findings soon. In the meantime, I welcome the new males to our council meeting and hope our talk of the search for my mate does not offend. Perhaps we can speak of something else now?" she said with laughter.

"My Queen," says Ramieda, her advisor from the Southern lands. She put her smallest fingers together and dipped her head. "With respect, we cannot afford to wait on pursuing these possible suitors for you. We estimate that your marriage needs to occur before the cold season begins, certainly before the equinox." A low murmur of agreement beat at the young Queen's ears.

Gazing out the window at the fresh blooms of new life outside, she sighed heavily. So soon? That would only give her two more seasons before she would be married, barely half a rotation of the planet. She had hoped for more time. Given her concerns about her sister's possible advances and the rumors of unrest among her people, she was coming around to the idea of choosing a betrothed sooner than later... but *now*? She gave a weak nod of her head.

"The Narthals to the North have a son," Ramieda continued. You'll remember they are fifth-generation Healers and birth experts? Very respected. The son, Thamus, is said to have been raised well with hopes of marrying royalty. Their family has a long line of daughters and are thought to be good breeders. He has four older sisters, so is thought to have good chances of providing female heirs."

Wincing, the Queen saw her advisors turn toward her with wide eyes. *I must calm down. My mother would never show discomfort in front of the council.* Removing her hand from her forehead, she shook her head softly. She would have to be open to all inquiries at this point, for now.

"There is also the Widower King from Malador. He is still young enough, and your union would join our two realms. This is most desirable." Ramieda looked at her beseechingly.

"That old male? I hadn't thought of it. No... surely our realm is mighty enough that we don't need to obtain lands from my union? I'd really like a handsome young male from a good-natured family. Someone used to life at court who won't faint at the first sign of hardship. Perhaps someone I can hold a conversation with? Maybe share some common interests with? Is this too much to ask?"

"Majesty, with respect, the only interests you need to share are the desire to make princesses for the realm and the ins and outs of court life. Nothing else really matters."

Cheeks flushing as she stood up suddenly, her legs stiff and spine straight, her voice quivered with intensity: "Nothing else matters? I disagree wholeheartedly! This is my life. I have a right to love, a right to passion. I will not be alone and miserable in my own marriage! I want something different, not like..." Her voice faded and dampness formed in the corners of her brilliant blue eyes. The salt made them shine.

"I will have some say in whom I marry. Nay, I will *choose* whom I marry. You may arrange a ball and invite all you deem fit. Make sure there are several males who meet the standards I have set out for you. Do not disappoint me!"

Nostrils flaring and face red, her hardened eyes swept the room, causing all heads to bow down but one. One of the new assistants met her gaze, his mammalian brown eyes reaching into hers with an unknown heat. He smiled briefly then looked down modestly. Her racing heart suddenly calmed. Blinking once and turning away, she briskly exited the chamber, heading toward her private rooms.

Chapter 4- When They Were Girls (Then)

Emmeldine lay in her large plush bed with no desire to sleep. She tossed and turned, quieting only when she heard sounds from Alara's bed across the room. Alara talked in her sleep and had been fitful for the last hour. Emmeldine heard her cry out, "Dono! No! My Dono!" Poor girl was missing her father. Emmeldine straightened the thick covers over her petite body, smelling the musty scent of wool while absentmindedly running her fingers over the intricate embroidery.

As she stirred she began to feel colder. Pulling the blankets up to her eyes, she sighed heavily. Was what they had seen that day magic? What else could it be? What was Mother so worried about? There was a soft knock at the nursery door and she heard hesitant footsteps approaching in the dark.

"Yes?" she asked calmly. Princess Emmeldine had never had a reason to mistrust or fear anyone, so was not concerned about a late night visitor.

"Princess Emmeldine?" A soft male voice folded back the air between them, allowing her to imagine a face where there had been only hazy shadows. She pictured a handsome young servant boy smiling at her with friendly intent. "Princess Emmeldine, I was sent by your mother. She would like you in her chambers. She asks that you not wake Princess Alara. May I escort you m'lady?"

Emmeldine giggled at the courtly term and peeled back her covers briskly. She stood up immediately and straightened her thin nightgown, shaking her head at the robe the boy held out in offering; she was no longer cold. Following him into the hall, she saw him cast down his eyes and his cheeks redden intensely. She wondered why he was so shy? *Oh yes,* she remembered, *it is different for males than females. They are not encouraged to be assertive and confident like girls. Must be hard.*

Following the lad, she takes a moment to notice his details. He is taller than her, appears to be about the same age, and is pleasant to view. He has shoulder-length, curly brown hair, brown eyes that remind her of chocolate, and a thick frame. Odd that her mother sent him instead of one of her ladies or a guard. Odder yet that her mother sent for her at all. Queen Maraleine felt strongly about growing girls getting a good night's sleep.

Approaching her mother's chambers, Emmeldine heard voices radiating out like heat, dips and sparks of sound that were yet to take shape into meaning for her. Getting closer, words started to become clear. The servant boy's face continued to have the same pleasant smile with no discernable change of expression, as if he heard nothing. She imagined her ears were magical, intensifying voices cloaked behind brick walls. Emmeldine grinned and stopped at the door, expecting the boy to open it for her.

"Oh! M'lady, I should have mentioned sooner — the Queen asks that you wait out here until she's finished meeting with her lov... Uh! I mean, meeting with her advisor." He flushed even redder than before and turned his head from her. Emmeldine realized the deeper tones she was hearing must be Dono, and she tried even more intently to hear what words were being said.

"It's not right! You mustn't! Please Maraleine, see reason... I love you —*worship* you. You are my Goddess. Isn't that...."

Then the strong, higher-pitched tones of her mother: "Enough! I'm tired of.... Don't think... because... I must....magic is real...."

Emmeldine took a step back. Magic is *real*? She must have misheard! Perhaps mother had said "magic *isn't* real?" How was she hearing this, and what else was being said? She felt like she had just caught part of an intimate lovers' quarrel, and yet the servant boy and the guards nearby didn't seem to have heard a thing. What was going on?

The chamber door to her mother's private rooms

suddenly burst open, and Warrior Dono rushed past her. Emmeldine was surprised once again. His stocky muscular body gave off a scent unfamiliar to the young Princess, yet somehow she knew it was associated with lovemaking and babies. His dark eyes flashed at her light ones and looked away just as quickly, his lips not saying a word.

The guard gestured for her to enter, and she did so. The Queen Mother was standing at her window, peering out into the darkness. "Emmeldine. Come in, child." Her voice was quiet and pensive — not a tone her daughter was familiar with. "I'm sorry to wake you, but there is a matter we must discuss which I fear cannot wait another day. It's especially important that you not speak of this to your sister."

Emmeldine considered telling her mother she hadn't been asleep, but decides to keep that information to herself. One thing court life has taught her thus far is that one need not share *all* with others. Even with one's mother — even the Queen.

"Yes, Mother."

Maraleine gestured at an empty chair, a thick padded cushion embroidered with the family's royal crest of trumpeting moonflowers. It called irresistibly to Emmeldine's suddenly fatigued body. She sat. Emmeldine noticed her mother's thick golden hair was loose, and her curvy slender body was covered in only an underdress and robe. Her mind went blank when her mother's piercing green eyes flashed at her.

"As my oldest daughter and the only full royal one, you know I expect a lot of you. I am grooming you to be Queen. Not only that, I also love you. Very much. I hope you know I do." Maraleine's face crinkled kindly as she smiled.

Emmeldine's eyes watered and she clasped her hands together to keep from shaking. The late hour and the uncommon emotion from her mother were wearing at her. She was very confused about all she had seen and heard since the last moon, and her head rumbled with thunder.

17

"Daughter, light of my light, I must be able to trust you, to know you will always do my bidding and follow my decree. Do you understand?"

Emmeldine's head nodded instantly as if jerked by the marionette strings of agreeable puppeteers, yet her mind was screaming. *No! I don't understand anything! What is going on?*

"Yes, Mother."

"I was informed by Warrior Dono that his daughter came to him this evening, very distraught." The Queen eyed her daughter, and silence hung between them, urging Emmeldine to speak.

"Yes, Mother?"

"You know nothing of this?"

"I did not know Alara had left the nursery Mother, nor that her father had returned. I had my music lessons after the evening meal — perhaps she slipped away then? Are you angry with the minders?"

"Don't change the subject, Emmeldine! I am asking if you know what Alara went to Dono about?"

Emmeldine bit her lower lip nervously as her thoughts ran wild. Shall I tell her what we saw? Did Alara tell Dono? Emmeldine hoped her mother would tell her what Alara had said without having to disclose her own activities, lest she be scolded — or worse.

The Queen shook her head and raised her eyes, studying her daughter intently. "Apparently, Alara told her father that she saw magic today. She said you two were wandering the castle and saw flashes of light and heard magic words. Dono was quite concerned, rightly so. He was concerned that you were fooling your sister, or perhaps even trying to scare her."

"Oh no, Mother! I am always kind to Alara. I have no reason to take aim at her; she is just a child. Besides, her company is often amusing — and I do love her so."

"Of course you do, Emmeldine. You have a large, loving heart like your father. And some of my good sense, I hope. So did something unusual come across your path today? Anything you would like to tell me about?"

Emmeldine briefly considered telling her mother all, but she remembered the tingle she'd felt in her body. The wonder of all she had heard that evening made her decide against it... for now.

She shook her head wearily, "No Mother, nothing of note. I do tell Alara stories of magic and adventure... hopefully she understands they are just stories."

The Queen stared at her daughter, brow raised and lips drawn tight. Finally her face melted into a taut pink surface and a twinkle returned to her eyes. "Of course! That must be it. Well daughter, you do need your sleep. Best you be off, my love." The Queen rose and embraced her firstborn, then turned away and gestured to her lady to help her to bed, thus silently ordering Emmeldine to exit her chambers. Which she did.

Chapter 5- Learning It (Now)

A frenzy of activity swept through the palace as preparations were made for the ball. The higher-born women were busy planning and scheming suitable matches for their beloved Queen. Nephews and sons were considered, and a long list was built. Weavers, artists, musicians and cooks alike were hired by the dozens to prepare a spectacle for the event thought to finally lead to Queen Emmeldine's betrothal. While the realm buzzed like a healthy hive, Emmeldine was hiding in its inner depths. The Queen Bee was worried.

"Is there any news of Alara?"

"No, My Queen. Not since our scouts spotted riders bearing the crest of her inherited estates north of Merwood. Nothing since."

"Are you certain? I sense something unsettling... I feel..." Emmeldine dropped her head and closed her eyes, trying to focus. "I feel energy that is... not pleasant. It's not of this realm. Is that possible?"

Shaima looked at her Queen with enlarged eyes and tight lips, then sighed heavily. "Yes, I dare say it is." The two women's eyes locked, wrestling silently until Emmeldine turned away.

"I know you think this is my fault, that I could have prevented my sister's betrayal somehow. Or that if I had enlisted magic sooner, none of this would be happening. You did warn me, after all."

"My Queen, while I enjoy certain blessings bestowed by the Goddess, it is you who was born the ordained ruler. Your word is sacrament, not mine."

Emmeldine suddenly turned back, eyes flashing. "Still. You knew — you always know. How is that?"

"I think you understand more than you realize, my Queen. So far, nothing is really happening. We know Alara has hostilities toward you and that she would like to rule.

We ascertain that she has obtained magic, although we do not know how, and that she has plans to use it against you. This is all."

"That is certainly enough to have me quite alarmed. So what do I do? Just sit here and wait? And what to do when she does come? How do we protect ourselves against this unknown force? What if the Fairies don't return?" Emmeldine realized she was wringing her beads till the strand was near bursting. She took a deep breath, relaxed her grip, and let them hang loose in her hand.

"I can teach you some now, My Queen. I think you know you have the power inside you. The signs have been there all along."

Emmeldine didn't bother to ask what signs. She knew.

Focusing on the feather, she studied the light tuft tickling her fingers, pleased by the pure white of it. The connection to the bird upon which it once resided resonated through her as she pictured it in flight, graceful and serene. The feather rose. Up, up as if caught in a current, yet the room was still. Her mouth stretched wide, her eyes sparkling as they followed the ascent of the soft, enchanted feather.

"Very good. That only took you a short time. I think your potential for magic is great, my Queen. You have the gift, of which I am not surprised."

"Is it a gift or a curse, Shaima?" the Queen asked softly as she stares up in wonder, eyes wide and mouth agape.

"There is much more you can do, Emmeldine. Your mother was not willing to access her power herself, only to let me funnel it for her. And rarely that. If you are brave enough to learn the ways of magic, you can be very powerful indeed. There is no reason to fear it. It's up to you whether the power is wielded for good or bad."

"Funny, I'm only considering using magic because

Alara is. Yet magic is what tore us apart...in one fashion or another. She was against, it you know."

"I know. Or rather it was her father, Dono, who was. I think she was just a child trying to please her parent. It happens every day. I used to feel so badly for that girl, vying for a place both in the palace and in her father's heart."

"I always tried to help her. I loved her very much."

"Yes, I know you did."

Chapter 6- Becoming A Woman (Then)

Time passed. Emmeldine's body grew and changed the way young people's will. Her ability to birth was marked by menses and a curvier frame. She became physically stronger and weathered many emotional turmoils, which led to growth of a different kind. Along the way, she started to make some inquiries into the mysteries of life. Her life felt exceedingly mysterious.

It's during this time that Emmeldine began wandering in the woods. She had been granted more freedom now that she was close to maturity. She got several hours a day to roam as she wanted, as long as she reported in to her mother before the evening meal. After years of studying and constant obedience to propriety, she found this more than refreshing. She was bursting with life.

The crackling crunch of the leaves satisfied her feet through her sturdy boots. The sound was rather pleasing — a audible force that produced no harm — like music. Reaching an open glen of the greenest green grass and rainbows of indigo, vermillion, and chartreuse flowers, she raced to untie her laces and tossed her boots down roughly, flinging herself onto the soft earth. Bliss! Leaning back, Emmeldine rubbed her feet on the smooth soil and watched a tiny white butterfly flap across her view. Glorious! Thinking about the power of the world, she marveled at the intricacies and detail the earth had to offer. Mother *is* wrong, magic is all around us. How can she fail to see the beauty of creation, of life?

Emmeldine thought about an interaction she'd had with her mother several fortnights previously.

"Mother, might there be something to the notion of magic? Perhaps it isn't something unnatural or alarming, but more an extension of the world we already know and understand. I see the hummingbird fly or see an ailing woman suddenly healed, and I can't help but wonder."

Emmeldine looked up into her mother's stern face and smiled at her with a tenderness only a child can show her life bringer, as if she were saying "thank you." Queen Maraleine's stony face softened as she reached out to touch her daughter's hand.

"These are dangerous thoughts, Daughter. I love that you see the beauty and mystery in the world, I really do. I just fear for you. Many great women have been brought down in their quest for magic. Any sort of power, if wielded unwisely, can be dangerous. Why should magic be any different?" With a final pat of Emmeldine's hand, she turned away and went back to her desk to look through the many papers that needed her signature.

Emmeldine's mouth gaped and her eyes widened. "Then you admit magic *does* indeed exist? That the stories are true?"

"That's... not what I said, Daughter. I am weary of this conversation. Please go resume your studies, I have work to do." Without another glance at her daughter, the Queen waved her hand dismissively, and Emmeldine was left alone with her thoughts.

Emmeldine was jarred from her reverie when suddenly, she heard soft rustling and realized the leaves along the edge of the glen were being disturbed. Jumping up, she reached for the dagger tied to her back. Prepared in the ancient art of self defense, her fingers gripped the golden handle as she called out in a calm, clear voice, "Who goes there?"

"Ooh, child! I didn't mean to frighten you. It is just I, an old woman making my way home." Suddenly a stooped figure appeared from the dense brush, carrying a bundle, as if returning from the village for supplies.

"And you would be?" Emmeldine fought the urge to correct the woman: *I am no child.*

"I am called Tatarnya, Child... and I know who you are."

Emmeldine winced, "Oh, do you?"

"Yes, future Queen Emmeldine."

Future Queen Emmeldine? She'd never heard that one before. While it was inevitable that she would someday be Queen, it was not often vocalized by others. Something about admitting the current Queen would someday be gone did not seem acceptable in courteous society. Eyeing the disheveled old woman, however, Emmeldine did not surmise that "courteous" was a word often applied to her.

The hunched figure drew closer. "Tell me Child, when you look at me, what do you see?"

"You may call me Princess Emmeldine, not *Child*." Emmeldine didn't really care what someone called her when she was wandering around in the woods, but she didn't quite know how to respond to this woman. She tried to buy herself some time. What did she see? Well, the woman was obviously very old, her back was curved, her hair was grey, and her skin sagged around her eyes like a waterfall. Yet... that was not what the woman was asking. What information did she seek? Emmeldine looked down into Tatarnya's moist, grey eyes and felt a questioning there. She pondered this.

Leaves whispered as a light breeze picked up, and Emmeldine sensed the earth waiting for her to speak. She didn't understand why this conversation was so important, yet somehow knew unequivocally that it was.

"I see someone who has lived a long time. Perhaps someone who knows things?" She hesitated.

"What kinds of things might I know, Child?" Her pale eyes squinted, never leaving Emmeldine's face.

"Things *I* want to know? Answers to mysteries? I...don't really know."

The Crone's eyes bored into the young princess, seeming to assess her merit and worth. After a great pause, she spoke.

"But you do know, don't you? You've always known."

Emmeldine shivered.

"Magic?"

"Yes, Child. Princess Emmeldine. Future Queen of Trimeria. You know magic is *real*. Would you like to learn more?"

"It seems you already know what I want. Need I even speak?"

"I do like a good conversation. It isn't often I have a guest as lovely as you. Won't you come inside?"

Emmeldine was startled, realizing they had wandered slightly during their discourse and were now in front of a small home on the far side of the glen — a mere shack, in truth. The wood was woven together and the roof was of thatch. The windows were but open holes and the furniture beyond appeared modest. They entered.

Chapter 7- Back At The Ball (Now)

Finally, the preparations for the ball were complete, and the Queen reluctantly ready to meet her suitors. It wasn't that she didn't want male companionship; on the contrary, she thought about it quite often. She longed for the male touch, but was terrified of a poor match. She wanted love.

Her ladies adjusted the flowing pleats of her long gown — the shimmering, icy blue fabric making their pale hands appear to almost glow with ethereal light. Emmeldine's red hair was up in intricate braids, framing her large, intensely blue eyes and rounded upturned nose perfectly. She excused her attendants and went to her large floor-length mirror alone, scooping up her jewelry from a small table along the way. Standing before the mirror, she carefully took the necklace she had chosen to wear and pulled it over her head gently. The multi-colored jewels sparkled against her modest bosom and flattered both the dress and the wearer. She had first removed her plain wood beads that she'd worn every day since her mother's gifting of them, but later thought to put them back on, tucking them under her gown. She hadn't taken them off for a moment since her mother passed into the unknown, and it felt wrong to remove them now. It seemed like mere days since they had spoke of it. "This necklace was given to me by my mother and passed down through each generation of women before her. It marks our power of birth and creation. When the time is right, after the occasion of your first menses, I will ceremonially gift it to you, thus marking the miracle of your ability to bring new life into the world. These ancient wood beads will hold your power for you until you need it." While her mother's turquoise eyes stared intensely into hers, Emmeldine thought she was just being poetic at the time. Shaking her head gently, she resumed adjusting her other jewels, bracelets and rings, but kept her ears bare of adornment. That would come soon enough.

Chapter 8 - What She Learned (Then)

Emmeldine nearly had to duck inside the Crone's hut, so low was the thatch roof. Straw hung and brushed the top of her head, sending a shiver slivering down her spine. She felt as if fingertips had swept across her. There were many jars, bottles, and small wooden boxes of various sizes. Animal pelts were piled in the corner: soft, dense brown furs, and thick fluffy white that her fingers longed to touch. Animal bones were scattered about as well, the skulls staring ominously through their empty sockets. Her nostrils flared as she picked up the scent of blood and herbs. Was this woman a Witch?

"Thinking I'm a Witch, are you?"

Emmeldine jumped at the old woman's raspy voice that vocalized her thoughts so exactly. She weakly shook her head.

"The line between Healers, Witches, Priestesses and magic users is thinner than you'd think, my dear. Many of the Healers you will meet actually have the ability to access magic, though they may not even know it. They do tend to be employed by highbred or royal families, so I imagine that keeps their curiosity at bay. Priestesses, of course, are spiritual in nature. They serve the Goddess, whom they believe to have created all womankind and modeled us after herself. That sounds like some kind of silliness though, doesn't it?"

Emmeldine gasped — she had never heard such heresy!

"I do agree about the "female only" part, though — males cannot be trusted with either healing or magic in any form. Their emotions are unstable and they are likely to do more harm than good. These days, I hear men are assisting the women. I suppose that is well enough as long as they don't get ideas of working on their own."

"My mother doesn't think men should work

alongside women. She thinks them too weak."

"Aye, smart ruler your mother is. You will learn."

Emmeldine didn't even realize she was shaking her head softly as Tartanya continued on.

"For most folk, the use of magic is thought to be fantasy only: the ability to make that which is not come forth, defying the laws of nature and the Goddess herself. Some families have historical knowledge of magic use handed down from their great-grandmothers and keep their beliefs to themselves. I believe you know some of these families, hmm?"

Emmeldine thought about this, but once again the old woman continued, as if not really interested in what the princess had to say.

"Witches are women, and occasionally men, who dabble in the other three on their own with no training and no supervision. They might heal, speak with the spirit realm, or attempt to manipulate the elements. So knowing whether any given "Witch" is of noble character or not is not always immediately possible. As you may know, it is not against the law to be a Witch, but Witches are usually looked down upon and often remain hidden. It could be quite challenging to know if someone is truly a Witch."

Tartanya eyed the young woman, taking in her rough breeches, her solid cotton tunic, her animal hide belt cinched around her tiny waist, her fiery red hair tied back tightly in a single braid. Emmeldine wiped at the dirt on her cheek and tried to straighten up, but was rudely reminded of the low ceiling and settled for a slight bend in her knees.

"Please excuse my poor manners Child, you should have a seat." Emmeldine suddenly saw a chair to her side that had previously evaded her notice. She sat.

"Tatarnya was it? Yes, Tartanya, what may I do for you? I'm afraid I don't understand your interest in my company unless it is to ask a royal favor.... or perhaps it's just that you are lonely?"

Laughter, thick and hearty, bellowed out of the Crone

as she pulled up a bench from under some pelts and sat down stiffly. "Lonely? Oh, Child, Princess Emmeldine, no. I am never lonely. How could I be? I am surrounded by my friends. My family. I am in constant contact with the plants, animals, and others creatures with which I commune. I am never lonely."

A flash of surprise crossed Emmeldine's face, and an unfamiliar emotion confused her. Lips pursed, she took a slow deep breath, letting it out more loudly than intended.

"Oh. I see."

"What of you, are you lonely?"

Emmeldine was taken aback. No one ever asked her about her emotions. Her desires were always considered and mostly met, but it was assumed that she was always happy and content. She lived in a beautiful palace with luxury and abundance: there was nothing to be unhappy about. Was she lonely? She thought about it. Her mother was often busy and usually distracted or distant. Her father was not around now that her mother had a new lover. The relationship between her and Alara was not what it had once been, and they confided in each other less and less. She did have her ladies, peers from her infanthood who attended her. Overall, Emmeldine realized she *did* feel unhappy — because she couldn't have conversations with those around her about the things she was really interested in. Like magic.

"Yes, I suppose I am lonely." A few tears welled up in her eyes and began to fall onto the dirt floor.

"What if I told you that you are never alone either Chil... Princess Emmeldine? Would you enjoy such information?" She waved her wrinkled hands around her stocky person, gesturing to all the odd objects shoved into her tiny home. Emmeldine shivered, wondering if she was about to learn some of the answers to her myriad of questions.

"I would love to know whatever it is you wish to tell me. Obviously you asked me here for a reason. Did you know I was coming?" She wiped her face and straightened up, looking the older woman right in the eye.

Ignoring the question, Tartanya leaned forward and grabbed Emmeldine's hands, squeezing them with a surprising amount of force but not hurting her. Emmeldine flinched in surprise at the unsolicited touch, then relaxed upon seeing the warm expression on the Crone's face.

Hours later, nearly dusk, Emmeldine left the Crone's hut and headed home. She was stunned by her encounter and all the old woman had told her. She thought about the part that had struck her the most.

"Every living thing is connected. There is energy that flows through us all, and when we tap into other energy, we can alter it. Such is healing. When you let go of "self" and truly connect with the injured person's hurt, you can fix it. You are never alone because your energy is connected to all others around you. Trees, animals, people — all life! Even the rocks. Everything!"

"Everything?" Emmeldine barely whispered, her throat tight and breath shortened. She could hardly believe what she was hearing. Yet somehow, she knew it was true.

"Yes, child. Back before your great-great-grandmother's time, there were people of magic. What we now think of as magical creatures, such as Fairies and Dwarves, were just other beings crossing over and co-existing in this realm. In fact, you come from a long line of such folk, your people were known as…"

"Wait! You're saying *I'm* a magical being? That we all are?" Emmeldine frowned and shook her head lightly.

"Oh dear, I think we've covered too much for one day. You have a lot to take in Child…Emmeldine."

Fatigue floated from her head to her toes, pulling her down as if a heavy weight had appeared. Yes, I've heard enough for one day. Yet she really wanted to know everything! Finally someone was willing to answer her questions and not just turn her away. With heavy eyes, she glanced at the small window and saw the sky change from brilliant blue to a hazy grey. She realized she had better get home for the evening meal, lest her mother become suspicious.

"Can I come again? Tomorrow?"

"Perhaps not tomorrow. But soon, yes. You come see me when the time is right. You will know."

"I will."

As she headed back to the castle, Emmeldine was lost in her thoughts, trying hard to make sense of all she had learned. She automatically headed toward home, barely noticing her surroundings. Emmeldine certainly didn't notice the figure watching her in the brush. She decided during her dazed journey toward the palace that Tartanya must be a mistaken old lady, probably desperate for attention. Still, she should visit her again. If only out of kindness.

Chapter 9- The Ball (Now)

Emmeldine felt a shudder of anticipation pierce through her core as she entered the ballroom. She thoroughly scanned the room full of handsome eligible men and realized it was finally happening: she would have a mate soon, fulfilling both her destiny and her desires. Emmeldine knew that all the candidates presented tonight would be well-bred young men who were peaceful and capable, men who had been taught in the arts of pleasure and companionship. The thought made her flush, and she squeezed her thighs together without meaning to. Deep breaths. Seeing the few unattached women present off to the side, she started to head their way: her ladies. Everyone bowed as Queen Emmeldine crossed their paths, and she noticed the sparkle and sway of the married women's ear-bobs. Their symbol of physical union with a male and the desirable result of such activity enticed Emmeldine to her advisors' sides.

"Look at that tall blond, My Queen!" squealed Ramieda close to her ear. "Has he got a mound on him! It's nearly indecent. Good for breeding, one might assume?" Quiet laughter.

"Really Ramieda, one shouldn't stare!"

"But Emmeldine, My Queen, what else are men good for if not to give us babies?"

"I don't even know where to begin. Seriously, you know I hope for more than that! You've been by my side since I was a wee babe myself. I want something… something different." Emmeldine frowned and her eyes narrowed. Sighing, she tried to relax her shoulders and loosen her jaw.

More whispering and laughter ensued as Ramieda turned to talk to the other young women beside her, while Emmeldine was whisked off by the elder partnered advisors to meet her intended.

Hours later, Emmeldine eyed her cushy purple velvet chair. Its plump cushions and intricate pattern of woven felt knots intermixed with vines of metal were very pleasing to the eye, yet she longed for her special seat for more practical reasons. Her feet ached like a farmer's after harvest. She thought she must have met not only all the eligible men in the realm, but half the others from afar as well. At first it was amusing to see who her advisors thought suitable for her. Tall, pale cousins who had brothers of their own who were *also* vying for her hand. The shorter, darker men from the same region in the North as Dono made her take pause. Those that were from families of power and those more modest but noteworthy. Noteworthy for their places in history as artisans, Healers, innovators and promoters of peace. Men who had been trained in the female arts and were obviously very sensitive and calm-natured. There were one or two who obviously resented being made to perform for their families — they had a thicker aura surrounding them and a dangerous look in their eyes. Emmeldine found this appealing. She was not looking for a doormat. She wanted a partner to rule with, to share the burdens and the joys.

Looking up from the current young male presented before her, she stifled a yawn and scanned the crowd. She saw her friends and ladies dancing joyfully. For them, this was a night of fun. They got to flirt and flaunt with no possible repercussion, and Emmeldine couldn't help but be envious. Her entire life had been so scripted, so ordained, that at times she thought about just going away and letting Alara rule. At least then, her little sister would finally be happy.

She shook her head to clear these thoughts. Realizing her handlers were giving her a break for refreshment, she wandered over to the crystal fountain spouting an alluring liquid of palest red. A serving boy abruptly ended his conversation with a male facing him and rushed to her side.

"Yes, My Queen? What can I get for you?"

"Thank you Laird, I would love a glass of small ale."

"Yes, m'lady."

The lad rushed to fill a crystal goblet and placed it on the table before her. She lifted the glass, surprised at its weight, and inhaled deeply as the rich earthy tones smelling of berry and spice tickled her nose. She rapidly took a few sips and a trickling of relief, a calmness, spread through her core and accumulated in her toes. Blessed ale. She giggled aloud.

Suddenly, the male who'd been talking to the serving boy turned around, and Emmeldine found herself looking up into familiar, sparkling brown eyes. Heat caressed her skin from within.

"My Queen! Are you free of your royal obligations at last? Has your duty been done?" His brown eyes twinkled and his lips turned up in a grin. Was he teasing the Queen?

Smiling, Emmeldine was pleased to see this familiar face. She took in his curly, dark hair that fell thickly to his shoulders. His thick, wide frame, broad shoulders, and muscular build were noticeable under his revealing tights and tunic. She blushed to see the bulge in his leggings and looked up quickly. "What is your name? I have met you several times I think; yet your name remains unknown to me."

"Pardon me m'lady. I should have made proper introductions the other day in the council chambers, but honestly I wasn't sure if you remembered me or not. I am Tharin. I served your mother the great Queen Maraleine as a lad, and I have been fortunate to pursue my education and find a position for myself with your advisor Elisia. I am pleased to be in your company again My Queen." Emmeldine detected a blush cross his broad cheeks and a flash of recognition shot through her.

"Oh, yes! You were the lad who led me to my

mother's rooms one night long ago. I thought you looked familiar."

"Yes m'lady." His eyes continued to twinkle and his grin widened. "I'm so pleased you remember."

Emmeldine felt a heat in her core and a tingle of excitement. Looking around, she saw the event's organizer gesture impatiently at her. It was time to resume the introductions. She felt like she wanted to talk to Tharin more, but wasn't sure what was proper. Well, what was the point of being Queen if she couldn't do what she wants at least some of the time?

"Tharin, would you come visit with me sometime soon? I would like to speak with you about your time here in the castle. And perhaps other things?" She felt herself blush. *What is going on with me?*

"I would be honored, m'lady. You look tired tonight and I know much is expected of you. Perhaps on the morrow?" Eyes dancing, he grinned at her enticingly then looked down quickly, gently biting his bottom lip.

"Yes, please. I will look forward to that."

"As will I."

The introductions resumed, and Emmeldine was expected to dance with the more prestigious suitors. While dancing with one of her ladies' cousins (whom she has already deemed too young and incredibly boring), she found herself thinking of Tharin. Funny that he should reappear after so many years, especially when she was looking for male companionship. She let out a large sigh as she remembered once again that she had to look for more than companionship; she must find a male to be the next King and rule beside her. Not a task to take lightly. The song blessedly ended and she was led away by Ramieda toward yet another possibility. Spotting grey hair and dull grey eyes, Emmeldine realized she was being led toward the Widower

King of Malador! Her cheeks flamed and she tightened her fists. The nerve! She was trying to figure out how to avoid engaging with him without creating a scene when she spotted yet another member of her cabinet heading toward her. This time it is Shaima. Her face was pale, her pace quick.

Heart racing, confusion settled in like an unwanted guest. *What is this about?*

Shaima reached her and leaned in to whisper, "Something is happening, we need to go immediately." Nothing further was needed for Emmeldine to understand. With a quick wave toward the King and her other advisors, it was understood she was needed elsewhere, and she strode rapidly out of the grand ballroom with Shaima at her side.

As the festive music faded and the sounds of frivolity dimmed, Emmeldine turned to Shaima for more information. "Is it the Fairies? Alara's grunts? What is it?" Her voice is calm, but her body was rigid with tension and her face almost yellow.

"There has been an intrusion in the dungeon. Several guards were killed and more yet are trying to hold something off. I'm not sure yet what it is, but there is a smell of burnt amber in the air and unnatural sounds coming from the caves below. It must be from Alara!"

"Yes, of course." Emmeldine's voice shook. "We knew this time would come. I thought the Fairies would have returned by now. Do you think they might have abandoned us?"

They continued to race toward the kitchens and descended the hidden stairs to the dungeons below.

"That's the trouble with creatures from other realms; there is no saying what they will or won't do. They seem to live by different rules than us. I've been praying daily that they return, and by the Goddess' will, they shall come."

Emmeldine didn't think it had much to do with the Goddess, but appreciated any sort of benevolent intervention. Trickles of ice crept across her heart as she contemplated how this night may end. She suddenly stopped as it hit her: an intense, unpleasant smell unlike any she had encountered before. Eerie flashes of light underneath the door before her assaulted her pupils. Blues, greens, and ethereal purples shot out the cracks, and low grunts alongside high-pitched squeals pierced her ears. She took a breath, fingered the beads beneath her ball gown, and reached forward to open the door.

Chapter 10 - Magic Is Real (The recent past)

"This is unbelievable, Shaima! Have I had this ability all along? Did my mother have it too?" Emmeldine smiled broadly, displaying a full mouth of small, pearl-like teeth as she poured water into a teapot using only her thoughts.

"Well... Yes. Although she hardly accessed it. As I told you, she used me as a funnel a few times. I think she was afraid of it. Also, she really was in love with Dono, you know. She tried to give up magic for him, but that didn't work out."

"What else can I do? How will I know?"

"Really, My Queen, you just have to think it to make it be. But you must *truly* believe it, and having a personal connection to your task makes it all the stronger... for instance, when you focused your love and knowledge of birds to make that first feather float. This is how healing works. Healers focus on what they know of the body system that is damaged, then visualize the defunct part repairing itself. Then it is so."

"Healers are magic users ?" Emmeldine asked, but realized as soon as the words were out of her mouth that she had heard similar information before. How had she forgotten?

"Well, yes and no. Many are and do not realize it, some know it quite well, and others only heal with their hands and the available science we currently possess."

Emmeldine realized she had been nodding her head since Shaima started to speak. "So I could heal?"

"It's quite possible, my dear. You won't know until you try, and it may happen in certain settings and not others. Magic is a tricky thing, as you shall soon see."

Emmeldine frowned as she eyed a small cut on her finger. She focused on it with all her might.

Chapter 11- The Dungeons (Now)

The door opened so slowly it was hard to notice any movement through the dusky haze. Heart thumping beneath icy skin, Emmeldine could barely breathe as her damp fingers gently pushed a little harder. When the thick wood had noticeably moved forward, she started to see more of the lights. Shots of reds and oranges joined the blues and greens, their beauty almost distracting her from the smell. Suddenly the odor hit her fully and her nose wrinkled in disgust. *Such a strong scent!* Her eyes widened, and Shaima's bony fingers grasped her by the elbow. The door opened enough to see two guards lying on the floor before them: one male and one female, both dead. There were no signs of wounds or bodily fluids — just vacant eyes illuminated eerily by the chaotic light show, proving their spirits had gone. Shaima uttered a quiet prayer as Emmeldine shakily advanced, clearing the door.

The air was hazy, as if smoke has recently been present. Emmeldine stifled a cough as she quickly scanned the room. The lights appeared to be pulsing out of the far left corner of the large dank chamber. The unnatural silence chilled her. The underground space was cavernous and Emmeldine could not see the opposite wall in the gloom. Only the ethereal colors coming from the corner provided light. Shaima slid up beside her and they both gestured to the corner at the same time. They slowly crept toward what little they could see. Large crates draped with various cloth and rope were piled high against the wall, and random items were strewn about. Suddenly a rat scurried across the Queen's foot, and she bit her lip to trap the cry of surprise erupting from her throat. Her sound came out like a quiet, yet high pitched squeal and she froze as a shot of green light darted past her foot and hit the rat. It *exploded*. Both women froze in place, and Emmeldine experienced something she had never truly felt before. Fear.

Heart racing, she slowly turned her face enough to see Shaima, seeking guidance. Shaima's eyes darted to the left. Her heart raced even faster as she saw a dark figure behind the boxes forty strands in front of her. The being appeared short but wide, possibly muscular. She felt a tingling in her head and fingers and unconsciously began to rub her fingers together. Glancing down, she saw a white light seemingly coming out of her fingertips. Her nails glowed. Before she could make sense of it, the creature lumbered toward them. Her whole body shook and before she could think what to do, the creature rushed forward and her fingers instinctively shot up, aiming straight at it. The white light intensified and a wave of it raced out to the being, appearing to hit it right in the torso. It collapsed and was still. Shaima grabbed the Queen's arm. "Are you unharmed?"

Emmeldine slumped to the floor, her entire body shaking uncontrollably. Shaima wrapped her arms around the Queen and squeezed comfortingly. The eerie-colored lights had gone out the second the creature hit the ground, but white light continued to glow from her hands. She stared silently at her limbs for a moment, then spoke so quietly Shaima tilted her ear closer, despite their bodies still being entwined.

"What is this? What is happening to me?" Emmeldine trembled and suddenly, all her muscles relaxed at once. As she started plummeting to the ground, Shaima reflexively wrapped her into the folds of her body, preventing her from hitting the cold, hard floor. The Queen was still. Shaima hurriedly reached about in the dark for a pulse... and found one. Her brave, strong ruler had merely fainted.

After abandoning her Queen in the basements to go find help she could trust, Shaima eventually got Emmeldine back to her private chambers. She waited for her to wake, both to comfort her as well as discuss the events of the evening. Shaima personally changed the Queen into a sleeping gown, gently wiped her face and limbs with a moist rag, then combed out her long hair as best she could. The sounds of her pupil's steady breaths comforted her. Shaima herself dozed off, and was surprised upon rousing to hear bird calls and see sunlight sneaking in through the cracks under the thick curtains. She looked around and saw the young woman sitting up — eyes open, smiling.

"I did it, Shaima!" she excitedly whispered. "I defeated one of Alara's goons with magic! I nearly fail to believe it!"

Despite her exhaustion, fear, and worry for the future, the Priestess couldn't help but smile at this prideful young woman before her.

"Yes, yes... you surely did indeed."

Emmeldine went back to sleep until late into the morning, her court believing her exhausted from the ball that had gone late into the night. Shaima fell asleep in the chair beside her after being reassured her friend was well. When she finally woke, she frantically looked to the Queen's bed and her heart lurched to find it empty. Luckily, before her mind began to spin out of control, she heard a rustle and looked behind her to see Emmeldine standing with her back to her. She cleared her throat to alert the Queen of her wakened state. Emmeldine spun around.

"Shaima! Look! I can do it again, I can do protective magic!" Pale, elegant hands held out before her, Emmeldine focused her attention on her fingers. Suddenly, a white light began to glow. She looked up at her longtime advisor — her friend — and glowed with more than power, but with pure joy.

Shaima's body began to tingle all over. She found it hard to breathe deeply enough. Her skin turned cold. *What had she started? What had she done?*

Chapter 12 - After The Crone (Then)

Young Emmeldine sat in her chamber, having recently transitioned from the nursery to a full suite of her own. The plush purple chair was as comfortable as it was elaborate, yet she couldn't help but squirm. She had been appointed several of her own ladies in waiting now that she was of childbearing age and training to be the next Queen. She was expected to have female companions whom would later become her advisors if they proved themselves true. Her closest friend, Daria, had left the chamber a while ago and Emmeldine had been fretting ever since, wanting to tell her about her encounter with the Crone. She needed to talk to someone about what had happened, but it felt so unreal. She hesitated to sound crazy, or worse yet, to be wrong. Maybe she had misunderstood what happened, could she have been dreaming? Emmeldine thought over every word said in the hut, her head hurting with possibility. What had the Crone been about to say at the end? About people of magic and the people here now? So curious.

A creak and a groan alerted the Princess to the return of her friend. Daria entered swiftly, carrying a tray of colorful tiny cakes and juicy fruits. Her curly black hair bounced against her shoulder blades and she grinned from ear to ear as she looked at Emmeldine, her blue eyes sparkling.

"I talked the kitchen into an early tea service! They let me take the snacks and let the lad a few strands behind me take the rest! Amazing what one can do when they are in service to the princess, the next Queen!"

"Hush!" Emmeldine giggled as she reached toward her, delicately plucking a tiny, frosted pink cake off the engraved silver tray. "You know my mother doesn't approve of my future status being mentioned. I think it scares her."

"I mean no disrespect. I am honored to serve you, both as a friend and as a lady." Daria looked right at her and put her fingers together, giving a slight bob of her head. Looking up, Emmeldine caught the glint in her eye, and it was as if Daria's perfectly upturned nose and splatter of freckles across her face were reassuring her of their keeper's innocence. Daria was a good friend.

All the rest of that day, Emmeldine thought about going back to the Crone's hut. As the moon cycle progressed she hoped to get away, but it seemed as if every time she prepared to leave the palace grounds, something was required of her. Once her music teacher asked her to assist in Alara's lesson; another time her mother sent for her; and yet again she was needed elsewhere. Never could she go.

Suns and moons seemed to fly by, and the Crone started to fade from Emmeldine's mind. She had many other matters that suddenly seemed more pressing.

"Daughter! Your sister has been distraught and missing her father. I want you to play with her every afternoon between lessons and tea. Understood?"

"Yes, Mother." Emmeldine gave a brisk curtsey.

"Also, Reynaldo, your father, is returning to the palace. He wishes to spend more time with us both and especially you. He will arrive this eve. Please be prepared to greet him in the main hall. I'm sure he will be eager to see you."

"Father? Really? Oh, but it has been a long time, Mother! I have missed him so. I still don't understand why he's been gone. Did something offend?"

"I'm afraid it's more some*one*. Your father and I have had many disagreements during our union, and he has not been accepting of my... let's say... "friendliness" with other men. You see, Daughter, it is my right as Queen to bed whomever I choose. I think you're old enough to understand this now."

Cheeks blazing, Emmeldine looked down at her slippers. Plush, pale purple with delicately embroidered moons and stars stared back at her, mocking her with their simplicity.

"Over the years, I have had a lot of pressure on me to bring forth female heirs in order to secure the throne. Your father has failed to provide all but one to me. The rest, as you know, were male. Your father has mostly been spending time with his boys, luxuriating at one of our country estates while I'm left to rule an entire realm on my own. I get lonely."

Emmeldine couldn't bear to look up. She was mortified by this line of conversation, yet couldn't help but hang on to every word. Perhaps if she didn't move, her mother would tell her of many more things she had long wondered about.

"But now he has received word that I am unwell, and despite all the turmoil and distrust between us, your father does love me. I know he does... in his own way."

At this, Emmeldine looked up sharply and breathed in a gallon of air at once, almost coughing as she spoke, "Unwell? Mother? What do you mean?"

"I've often been tired, my love; my body is weak. I was with child a while back, and I did not want to alert you until I knew things were well. They were not. Now the child is no more and something has changed within me. I am consulting with my Priestesses and local Healers. I'm sure all will be well in time. Please, do not speak of this to anyone. A Queen must always present a strong front, Emmeldine — don't you ever forget that."

"Yes, Mother... I mean... no Mother. I won't."

"Emmeldine! Why aren't you playing with me anymore? I miss you." Alara didn't even try to mask the whine in her voice.

"Oh sweet sister, I am sorry! I have been ever so busy with one thing or another. Silly grown-up matters, really. Besides my own lessons, I am having to follow Mother more and more. Learning how to be Queen, I suppose."

Emmeldine paused upon seeing her sister's frown deepen and thought quickly. "I do want to plan a special outing with you! Perhaps I can introduce you to my new secret friend."

Alara suddenly beamed up at her. "A secret friend? Where? Who is it? Can we go now? Please?" Her golden ringlets bounce as she looks up at her big sister with hopeful, shining eyes.

"Not now I'm afraid, but soon. Perhaps on the morrow? I will have to ask Mother."

"Yes, yes please! Ask Mother now!" the child demands.

"Patience, Alara — you really must learn some patience."

Later that day, Emmeldine did go to see her mother, hoping to have tea with her in the Queen's chambers. She was let in after quickly conferring with one of her mother's ladies. Maraleine was in her bed, propped up by several large, fluffy pillows. Her skin looked sallow against her colorful sleeping gown and she appeared much too thin. Emmeldine stopped suddenly in surprise.

"Daughter. Come here, my beloved. I have something important for you." Maraleine waved her thin arm in welcome, and Emmeldine did as she was told.

"Mother! You don't appear well at all. What is the concern?"

"Don't fuss, Emmeldine. I will be well soon, just you wait. My Priestesses and Healers are taking good care of me, and I am feeling better already. More importantly, I wanted to see you because it is time I give you something special. You are almost a grown woman now, and it's time I passed down the beads for real, not just in ceremony."

"Your special beads, Mother? The lovely wood ones with the amazing carved design?"

"Yes. They were my mother's, and hers before. Handed down from great Queen to great Queen since near the beginning of time. And now they shall be yours." Maraleine gestured to a serving lad Emmeldine hadn't noticed in the corner of the chamber, and he brought forth a shiny silver box. The Queen opened the jeweled lid and pulled out a strand of brown beads which at first appeared simple. She gestured to Emmeldine to come closer and raised the strand up over her head. Straightening, Emmeldine lifted her hair out from under the light beads, shaking her red locks free. She gently lifted the beads and caressed their unique texture of smooth wood mixed with intricate, tiny carvings. They were stunning.

"Oh, Mother! They are special, aren't they? Are you sure, though? Shouldn't you wait till... till later in life? Surely you're too young to pass on things to me, won't you be missing them?"

Maraleine looked down and took a slow breath. After a long pause, she looked back up, her eyes swimming in shallow pools of emotion as she shook her head.

"No, it is time to pass them onto you. I shall enjoy seeing them on my beautiful daughter's neck. They hold the essence of our family line. Touched and worn by every woman of my direct line and now held by my own daughter. I couldn't want for more. I ask that you wear them every day, and touch them in times of trouble or turmoil. Let them bring you the love and light they have given me."

"If it pleases you Mother, I shall do so. Please request them back at any time and I will return them in haste. These are beads meant for a Queen, and I am not that."

Emmeldine gave a shallow curtsy toward her mother and saw her start to smile. Suddenly, a trumpet blast was heard through the open window, and the Queen's smile faded into a frown.

"It's your father — he has arrived."

Emmeldine quickly excused herself to go greet her father, completely forgetting there was something important she had wanted to ask her mother.

Chapter 13 - Healing (Now)

After dealing with as few royal duties as possible for the day, Emmeldine excused herself to her rooms, feigning exhaustion from the ball. In truth she was quite invigorated, feeling a pleasurable pulse radiating from her core throughout her body. She was whole in a way she had never been before. Earlier, she had met with Shaima briefly to further discuss the events of the previous night. While the young Queen knew she should be worried, she was full of excitement to finally see a magical creature with her own eyes.

"Shaima, I still can't figure it out, what was that creature?"

"I too am perplexed. I attempted to bury it myself after further examination, but the wretched thing had vanished. This is not surprising given its magical nature. I've been consulting my scrolls — the ancient wisdom of my mother's line — and have come up with some possibilities. The creature was foul, putrid smelling and unpleasant to view. I am guessing some sort of troll. They are known to be more sly and better at defense then that wretched fellow seemed to be, but I think it was still stunned from entering our world. Thank the Goddess it wasn't at full capacity or things might have ended poorly indeed."

"Full capacity? You mean it could do worse? Worse than killing off the guards and nearly killing us?" The Queen shivered and wrapped her arms tightly around her bosom.

"I dare say so. Magical creatures can be ever so powerful, especially when they are feeling strong emotion — and that beast was pure hatred."

"But why? Why would it hate us?"

"I don't know, my dear, I really don't know."

Emmeldine shivered and fingered her beads gently, staring at a silver sculpture on her bedside table without really seeing it. She felt a familiar sting in her eyes and quickly wiped at them.

"And what of the guards that died? How do we talk to their families? How do we explain their absences?" Looking up with red eyes, she found Shaima's firm gaze contained a few tears as well.

"Aye, indeed — this has weighed on me plenty for many reasons. I had to think quickly on this, and decided to trust Ramieda. She has come up with a story for the families about the guards dying loyally in the line of duty. Well, that part is exceptionally true. The actual cause of death, she is claiming, cannot be revealed so as to protect the crown. I hope you can agree with this?"

Emmeldine gave a weak nod of consent, her gaze returning to the sculpture. After a moment of silence, her eyes snapped back to her elder friend.

"And what of me? It appears I can do white magic. What does this mean for me? Am I a magical creature? A Healer? A...a Witch?" Emmeldine grabbed her beads and looked down, taking a deep breath that sounded heavy to the Priestess. Afraid of her own power.

Shaima looked over at her with wide eyes watering, overcome with emotion. She wondered if she should finally tell her? Was it time?

"Do you really want to know? If knowing will mean your life will change, and quickly at that?" Seeing Emmeldine's mouth open immediately, Shaima raised a hand toward her young ruler. "Wait, think a moment my dear, think hard. You are on the brink of war, you are charged with finding a mate, and you have discovered new abilities. Perhaps one should take some time to just *be*? You must feel whole in who you are as Emmeldine, as Queen. Then you can know what else makes up your being."

Finally the young Queen, so strong and steadfast, wavered. Lips pursed, eyes clinching, she collapsed into a heap on the floor of her chamber, crying violently. Shaima lowered herself slowly and reached her arms around that petite frame of strong femininity, comforting the most amazing girl she had ever known.

Several days had passed when Emmeldine entered her room briskly, relieved to be done with the evening's feasting and ritual. She sat down at her desk as she had for the last few eves and wrote in her book of thoughts. The tension slid out of her neck and shoulders as she further contemplated the events of the last moon cycle. Gently fingering her beads, a relief of sorts trickled through her, and her senses started to talk to her more deeply. There was a faint sound of muffled voices and music from the hall, reminding her of the constant hum of the evening life in the meadow outside the castle — busy, yet peaceful. Scents of roasted meats and hearty breads made her nostrils flare with pleasure and her belly growl plaintively. Once again, she had been too distracted to eat much that day. Just as she contemplated sending for food, there was a faint knock at her door. The guards had let someone through, so she knew it was safe to answer.

"You may enter."

A large, muscular figure with tousled brown hair and shiny warm eyes appeared. Emmeldine rose quickly, a large smile pushing her cheeks up and making her eyes sparkle.

"Tharin! It's good to see you! Please come in. I haven't seen you in days, not since..." She blushed and searched her mind for the words to express how she felt. So much had happened since they last spoke.

"Not since the ball. Yes, my Lady. I do apologize for not coming sooner; we had planned to talk further and my time has been taken by my duties to your cabinet. I hope you will forgive me?" He looked up with a crooked grin and crinkled eyes. Emmeldine giggled, a soft sound of bells and bubbles. Tharin bowed deeply, pretending to grovel. Her laughter thickened.

"You may rise," she laughed loudly, regally placing her hand on his shoulder. A spark of heat warmed her fingertips and he looked up immediately, their eyes locking. Emmeldine was startled by that hot, tingly sensation she had experienced when she last had spoken with this dashing male. It was more than pleasurable — it was *divine*. She noticed a small basket Tharin had brought filled with breads, cheeses and a small red cake shaped like a flower. "Is that for me? I find myself quite peckish just now."

Grabbing the basket he had left on the ground, he quickly handed it to her.

"Yes, I thought to bring you a treat. Something sweet to remind you of all that is delicious around you."

He looked down quickly, cheeks reddening to his ear tips. Emmeldine admired those pink, round ears and has the sudden urge to touch them with her lips. She shivered.

"Emmeldine...may I call you Emmeldine?" He rose and she nodded her head, their eyes staying locked together, as if embracing. His smile widened. "Emmeldine, I so relished our talk at the ball. I like your company. Would it be too forward of me to ask for some of your time? To visit you often?"

"I would most enjoy that. Yes, I think that best."

Chapter 14 - Father Figures (Then)

Emmeldine's stomach fluttered strangely as she hurried down the spiraling staircase toward the palace's main entrance. Her mother had promised to come down shortly. The chamber below was abuzz with activity as special preparations were being finalized to welcome back the King. It had been clusters of moons since Reynaldo had set foot on these marble floors, and many were eager to have the Queen's mate back in his rightful home.

Emmeldine thought back to the last time she remembered having an actual conversation with her father. They were in the south gardens wandering together. She clearly remembered the sensation of reaching her arm up to meet his giant hand, loving the feeling of her hand being lost within his. His long lanky body was very strong, and when they held hands and swung them, he had to barely shuffle his feet for fear of pulling her arm too hard. During these walks, they would sing songs from his home lands that were about animals or silly recounts of mischief gone awry. On this day, Reynaldo suddenly stopped singing and turned to her, an expression in his blue eyes and downturned thin lips that perplexed his only daughter. She squinted up at him, cocking her head.

"Emmeldine, dearest girl, there are hardships in life — times that others will try to hurt you. I fear you've been too... *protected* here in the palace. Your brothers are having such a very different childhood at our country estate. I would very much like to take you there. You could run, climb, ride and cavort in ways a young lass should. I fear to see you so limited, so confined."

"Why, father? Why don't I play with my brothers? I haven't seen them in ever so long. Is it because boys are bad? Were they naughty?"

"Oh no, not at all! They are lovely boys. They share and help each other, they are studying hard and ever so bright. Why, Treyu is almost a grown male now, and your mother is working to secure a good marriage for him. Ladin is close to your height and very good with horses and other beasts. Damin, the baby, is not so little anymore. He was born two solar cycles after Alara."

With that, Reynaldo's face had switched from a soft, open expression of love to a cold, hard frown. Emmeldine felt her shoulders tighten.

Clearing his throat, her father tried to recover from his dark turn of thought. "No — boys aren't bad at all. Anyone can have evil in their heart or do wrong; your gender doesn't change that. But you have probably heard of how things were very different long ago. When men had more power in the realm. Yes, it is true — there was more bloodshed and much war. Males do have the tendency toward aggression, you see. But... things are much different now. Over much time, our people have learned how to work with young boys and raise them in ways where their aggression is checked. Contained, even. I actually have great hope that men and women will soon be equals and that all males will be accepted everywhere for every purpose. Well, except they can't bring babies into the world of course. Women are definitely blessed by the Goddess with that gift."

Emmeldine's cheeks turned pink and she looked down at her toes, gently scraping the soft earth. She had so many things she wanted to ask her father, yet they had never spoken this way before; she felt unsure what to say next. The words suddenly fell out of her mouth.

"Does that mean my brothers will come live at the castle now, and you will be equal to mother in rule?"

Reynaldo laughed — a tight, unpleasant laughter that did not reach his eyes. "No, my dear daughter, I dare say not. Your mother does not share quite the same views as I. She believes women and women alone are blessed by the Goddess with good sense and strength of character. She fears if men are given power, we will go back to our old ways and much war will commence. I pray she is wrong."

He fell silent and walked a little faster. He had dropped Emmeldine's hand, and she scurried to keep up.

Near breathless from both motion and emotion, the young princess felt compelled to comfort the King, "I will pray as well, Father. I will pray."

Chapter 15 - Presents In The Present (Now)

Tharin was now seen around the Queen's chambers quite often, and she made no attempt to hide their friendship. Whispers and speculation abounded in the palace. Emmeldine struggled to contain the heat she felt around him, aching alone in bed at night for his touch. Confusion clouded her head. *Is it ok to give in to my desire knowing full well I cannot marry Tharin? What if we conceived a child? Why exactly can't I marry him, anyway?* The answers felt tangible and reclusive all at once, the logic behind them not quite making sense. In the meantime they took walks in the gardens, read poetry in the parlors, and taught each other how to play different instruments: she quite adept at the harp, he more inclined to the wood pipes. They never spoke of the future, and Emmeldine did not speak of magic or her newfound abilities. After Tharin left her every evening, she met with Shaima to practice her new skills and to strategize. It was on one such eve that the two women were sharing tea in the Queen's chambers.

"Mustn't we though, Shaima? The recent attack near Murwood reeks of suspicion! It is time to recruit others. You and I cannot hold off what is to come." The Queen shivered, unwittingly clasping her wood beads.

"I understand, my dear, I truly do. We must be wise, incredibly cautious in whom we involve. The older woman lowered her teacup and fixed her eyes astutely on her young friend. "Did you have anyone in particular in mind?"

"Yes well... Daria, for one. She has shown signs of openness to magic, and I trust her explicitly. It also seems wise to have several council members involved, so the council itself can be swayed should the time come for such things."

"Aye. You are becoming a wise ruler. It is always important to look ahead and plan accordingly. Daria is an excellent suggestion... perhaps Ramieda, too. I would also add Chloe and Sarsha. I see the gift there."

"Agreed. Shaima, speaking of looking to the future, well... I remember my mother mentioning a prophecy. I believe she was speaking to you? What was that about?" Emmeldine blushed a little and looked directly into Shaima's eyes.

"Goodness! How did you hear of that? We tried ever so hard to keep everything from you. Not in malice, of course, but to protect you. Yes, there was a prophecy. It was from the scrolls my mother passed down to me, lore from the words of the Goddess herself. It spoke of a time that would come when another female heir would be necessary to your mother's rule... that in order to bring balance and peace, a baby girl needed to be born after the daughter who would become Queen. The balance of the realm depended on it." Shaima's voice got quieter as she spoke, casting her eyes down at the end.

Emmeldine's own eyes widened as she listened, and she felt a lump in her throat float down to her heart and stick. Her mind started to swirl with the possible meaning of this. Shaima looked up at her with watery eyes and reached out her rough, wrinkled hand to take the soft, smooth one before her.

"How could you know this prophecy spoke of my mother's reign? Surely it did not refer to her by name?"

"You are correct, it did not. There were reasons we both felt it referred to her, signs you might say. Intuition. Prophecy is hard to interpret and harder still to move through with clear understanding. You mustn't think the worst or assume anything. Your mother felt she had to birth another daughter fathered by Reynaldo. Others might have viewed things differently. And then there is the notion of balance..."

"What do you mean?"

"Well... balance can be taken to mean equal portion, an even scale. Our realm here has enjoyed unprecedented peace and prosperity for a great many year. So what would balance mean for us? I am not so sure I would have made the choices your mother did. Blessed woman though she was." Shaima dipped her head reverently.

A long silence sat between them, its heaviness beginning to squeeze Emmeldine's skin and wiggle into her core. Finally she was able to speak in barely more than a whisper, "I honestly don't know what to say. I need to absorb this. In the meantime, let's invite the small group of women to meet with us nightly to learn and practice defensive magic, and pray we do what is wise. I'd like to be alone now, Shaima. Thank you."

"Of course, my dear. I will see to the arrangements. We shall practice on the morrow." Shaima slowly rose, resting a wrinkled hand spotted with life on the firm shoulder of her friend. She gave a reassuring squeeze before turning to walk back to her own chambers.

"Shaima! Wait! One more thing, although, honestly, I feel as if my head may burst. It bothers me so to think of magical creatures wishing me harm. Why would they come here with mal intent? Why partner with Alara against me?" Emmeldine's face had turned stark white and she shook all over.

Shaima rushed back to the Queen and wrapped her arms around her. She made shushing noises as one might to a small child and squeezed her tight.

"Dearest Emmeldine, I really do not know. I can speculate that certain groups of magical beings are using Alara to enter our realm. There is reason to believe there has been great division in their lands and some of the beings want to come here. I really don't wish to speak of this anymore, as it will only be speculation. Please know that all will be well, we are on the side of good, and love, and all the Goddess represents. We shall prevail."

"Thank you. It is intensely uncomfortable to feel hated. I shall try not to dwell on this." Tears started to rain down Emmeldine's cheeks as they pinkened.

"Please do, my dear. Please do. You are greatly loved. Of this I am certain."

Emmeldine tossed and turned at night, wondering if Alara was the second daughter born that the prophecy spoke of. And if so, how was she meant to bring balance to their realm? Was she meant to bring evil to counteract all the good they had known? Emmeldine tried not to fret, and prayed to the Goddess fervently to lead them toward ongoing peace and prosperity.

A moon cycle of days and one eve passed. As the murky greys and violets faded into deeper inky black depths, Emmeldine sat on her balcony. Tired eyes took in the lush plant life below without really seeing. She sighed heavily and took several deep breaths. Clenched fists relaxed as she slowly exhaled. She found herself frequently wondering what she would do about the myriad of concerns weighing on her shoulders. Calming techniques were becoming a mandatory part of her evening rituals. Large, strong hands grasped her waist and gently pulled her toward a firm, warm body. A familiar scent nestled in her nostrils. *Tharin.* The heat of his touch paired perfectly with the dying embers of light drifting from the sky, like weeping rays of possibility. His long, hard body leaned into hers, and a soft wet pressure teased the back of her neck. He was kissing her! Starting to pull away even as pleasure flooded her veins, she gave in as his grasp tightened, and she relaxed into his arms. He sighed softly.

"Tharin, we mustn't. We can't…"

"Oh? It seems we can. Do you like this?" He nibbled between her collarbone and shoulder blade with a little more pressure.

"Oooo… oh yes. Oh please.. Please, stop." She pulled away.

"Stop? Is that really what you want?"

"I…I don't know. There is so much going on right now, I…"

She looked up into his eyes and her own began to water. He reached out to touch her hand.

"I'm sorry, dear Emmeldine, please, please don't cry. I know there has been something distressing going on and I wish you could tell me. I know there have been some sort of secret meetings…"

"You do? How could you know?"

"I have been the eyes and ears of these castle walls since I was a small child. I can't help but pick up on things."

"I see." She pulled away, her long, loose hair swaying before her as she shook her head from side to side. Looking down at the worn stone beneath her feet, Emmeldine's eyes stung and her body tightened. A cold coil grasped her insides and she knew she had to be alone, immediately.

"Excuse me, Tharin — I must go. Rest ye well."

Pain flickered in his eyes as they widened, but since she did not look up, she missed his startled expression. Briskly turning away, she rushed through the chambers, biting her lip as she went off to look for the one person she could truly trust.

Unsuccessful in her quest, Emmeldine went back to her now empty chambers to ready for slumber. Confusion clouded her thoughts. *Why do I suddenly feel so leery around Tharin? Perhaps I am afraid of him finding out about our recent doings. About magic.* Shaking her head lightly, she took a deep breath and picked up her brush.

While stroking her hair, Emmeldine thought of the strong women she was training with, nimble and determined.

Chloe was small and fair like her, quick like a bird of prey. She could be in and out of an opponent's reach before a breath fell from her lips. Then there was Marianee, thick with sun-bronzed skin and a determination like no other. She not only trained hard physically, but seemed to instantly connect to her inner spirit and embrace it in a way that allowed her to start using magic through her tools — her favorite being a spear. (Emmeldine wondered if she had practiced before, but was hesitant to speak of it.) Sarsha was reserved — resistant, even — but she too started to improve by the end of the second session and showed potential. She was a logical thinker, and seemed to figure out tactics and be able to plan ahead better than most. The only time Sarsha's blue eyes would sparkle was after a successful attempt at magic, her golden-red head held proudly on her lithe frame. Surprisingly enough, Ramieda joined their group and showed natural ability as well. Apparently, Shaima had seen it in her all along.

Shaima, of course, was the connector: helping all the women amplify their gifts and contain them. Emmeldine felt hopeful that with such strong, capable women by her side, she could fight back whatever was to come. The anonymity of the faceless foe was certainly a weight wrapped and wringing around her, squeezing tight. She struggled to breathe.

Chapter 16 - Another Male (Then)

Reynaldo stayed for quite some time and Emmeldine basked in his attention. Every day they would go on strolls, have picnics, or go horseback riding into the countryside. Her sister, however, was not so pleased. Not only was she jealous, but she was deeply hurt. Her beloved older sister seemed to have little time for her, and her own father was nowhere to be found. Their mother was still in her own chambers more often than not and the whispers and speculation spread like Fairy fire. Alara began to be sulky, quiet — not the bright, sparkling girl that ran the palace halls like a banshee.

One gloriously sunny day, the Queen Mother was making a rare appearance in the garden courtyard. Royal rays of light seemed to pour down on the entire family during this rare occasion where they were all gathered together. Alara tried to wait patiently while her mother spoke with Reynaldo quietly as they sat on a marble bench. Alara was sitting near a large flower bed full of the royal colors. Red rampsies, purple moondrops, and golden lanterns glistened with their nectars. The scents were intoxicating.

Emmeldine was sitting next to her father, leaning her head on his broad shoulder. Alara felt her eyes narrow and her lips turn down, a feeling of tight heat spreading through her belly. Suddenly she saw her chance: Reynaldo stood up stiffly and brushed his pants off, then turned as if to walk away. Alara sprang up and ran toward her mother. Her face had just enough time to change into an expectant smile, eyes shining, when she registered that Emmeldine had slid in closely to their mother and the two were now talking quietly with bowed heads, bodies bent toward each other, obviously disinviting others from joining them. Alara stopped cold in her tracks, her whole body chilled with stiffness. Slowly she forced herself to turn around, and slower still she headed away from the cozy pair on the bench. Her heart ached with each step.

The next day, both girls woke at nearly the same time in separate parts of the castle. A large cheer rang out and they both sprang up in their beds with a start. Alara ran to the window, eyes wide and heart racing. Emmeldine stayed sitting up in bed, slowly rubbing at her own bleary eyes, thoughts trying to catch up with her body. Alara's eyes widened at a most unusual sight. A large group of women with several brawny men among them was entering the courtyard gates. They wore brown animal hides and carried bows, swords and other objects of inflicting harm. Alara had only heard tale of such instruments, as these things were not usually allowed within the palace walls. The women were well-muscled in a leaner way than the men, and slick with sweat between the large swaths of dust covering their persons. All of these brown-haired, dark-eyed people were moving triumphantly — heads held high, strides purposeful and long. Just as she thought she had viewed them all, Alara saw one last male enter the courtyard. Her heart dropped to the floor and she nearly forgot to breathe. It was her Dono.

It was years before Alara truly understood what had happened. She would learn that there had been a threat at the Northern borders: bands of misfits were attacking small villages. She eventually would realize that a dozen or so men had formed together against the laws of the land, becoming an organization of sorts. This group was adamant that men not only deserved equal rights, but were in fact the superior gender. The men planned to use their brute strength to prove their position and to recruit more males to their cause. Royal spies caught wind of this plot in time to stop it from spreading from the border region. The Queen had sent a select group of her fiercest defenders to take them down. Which they did.

Alara found her teachers the best source of information and decided her instructor Malga, who loved to discuss history and social structure, was her best chance of understanding more about the adults in her life. One day, Malga told her about the last King to spread his anger and malice over the lands.

"In very early times, warring was common, and men led the charge. As a community, the peoples came together and decided that the male gender was too frail emotionally, that they could not control the animal inside themselves. It was decided by the women and all the elders that men should be subdued and women should rule. The King at this time was Damien Tharlock, and he was so devastated by the loss of both his sons in battle that he reluctantly agreed to abdicate the throne. His cousin Trinna Tharlock was placed as high ruler, Queen of Trimeria. It is said that the Goddess herself aided in this change of power."

Alara gasped. "the Goddess herself? I did not think the Goddess ever came to our realm in a visible form?"

"Well there is dissent about this I must say, but the royal history books teach it to be true, and your own mother believes it."

Alara blinked and tried to clear the cloud forming in her mind. "Thank you Malga, please continue."

"This started a chain reaction through the lands — uprisings in some, intricate plotting and conniving in others, but the result was the same. Over a relatively short period of time, males lost or gave up their positions of leadership and women took over. Queen Trinna was thought to be a just and wise ruler. She helped the villages and townships to form peaceful leadership and transition relatively smoothly into non-aggressive ways of handling conflict. Of course there was some resistance and some fighting as a result, but that only went further to prove the point that men were too aggressive for their own good and needed womankind to step in and help them correct the error of their ways."

"My goodness! How then is my father allowed to fight? Although he is kind and loving and wonderful, well, he is male…"

"Yes my dear. Over time we have perfected trainings

and put systems in place to teach certain men to express and control their emotions, to be able to use their brawn only when it is truly needed. It has come in quite handy, as males are still the physically stronger sex. Of course we have many strong women now, too."

"Yes! My father works with women who are tall, muscular and seem very capable physically. They act as if they are his superiors even though I thought they held the same position?"

"Well, I think that is something you will learn more about in time. Enough for today, child. I know learning the ways of our realm can be confusing. You are a lucky young woman though; your mother is the Queen and your father an enlightened male. You are blessed by the Goddess for sure." Malga patted her hand and turned away, excusing her pupil from the lesson room. She never saw the tears pooling up in the young girl's eyes as she slowly walked away.

Alara was beyond overjoyed at her father's arrival — she was *ecstatic*. She pranced around the grounds with him like an eager pup with a large, wide smile and braids flapping. At first she was solely basking in his attention and did not ask much, but over time she started to let her curiosity wander. On one particularly peaceful afternoon, they were wandering the northern gardens — primarily tall, thick shrubbery that provided a sense of privacy. They had stopped to rest on a marble bench and Dono was staring off into the greenery, a slight smile upon his face. Alara snuggled up close to him and rested her head on his broad shoulder. She loved that his scent was that of no other she had known and his shoulder so hard and large, practically shouting of strength to her. She felt him stiffen and she quickly looked up, seeing his pleasant expression turn downward and a crease form between his eyes.

"What is it Dono...I mean, Father? What's wrong?"

"Alara, my own blood, you are wise to read my feelings. This skill will get you far in our world. Pay attention. Never let your guard down. Beware those whose feelings are false."

"False, father? How can a feeling be false? Doesn't one either feel a feeling or they do not?"

"You would think so my child, but alas, it is not always so. Sometimes people will say they feel one thing, but show with their faces or bodies that they truly feel another. And sometimes people's actions do not match what they say they feel."

"Are you speaking of Mother?"

Dono flinched, "Alara, we must be careful when speaking of your mother. She is the Queen, the high ruler of the land. And her word is final here — we cannot afford to contradict her or do anything that will make her look foolish. This is why I stay away so much. She says she loves me best, more than Reynaldo, more than any... but she does not treat me as an equal."

"Yet you are allowed to fight with the women Warriors, are you not? Is not that a sign of respect? Perhaps even of love?"

"Ah, yes. There is that. I fought hard for the privilege of putting my life in peril to protect the crown. It is a position allowed very few males, and for that I am grateful. But you must understand, Alara — I *earned* it. I worked harder than anyone to learn my emotions, to control my primal urges, and to become the fastest, strongest fighter I could become. My position was not given to me as a gift from one lover to another — nay, it is mine by right!"

"I know father, I have learned about this in my studies." Alara sat up proudly.

His flushed face glistened in the sun as he scowled, wiping some forming moisture from his brow. Alara was surprised by her father's emotional outpouring; he was not usually very forthcoming about his relationship with her mother.

"And now *he's* here — Reynaldo." This was said with a strange tone Alara had never heard before, as if her father was both disgusted and amused all at once. Her father looked up at the sound of distant laughter and frowned.

"I see." Alara wanted very much to sound grown up, to be worthy of her father's mature conversation. "Well, Father, I am forever your loyal daughter. If you should ever need me to assist you in some way, to help further your favor, I would be ever so happy to do so."

"Alara, my love, that is all a father could ever ask. Thank you, my dear, I very well likely might do so in time. In time…"

That evening, both the Queen's lovers and their respective daughters were seated at the royal table for a large banquet.

The Queen rose.

"Dear friends and beloved family…"

Maraleine glanced first to her right at Reynaldo and Emmeldine, and then to her left at Dono and Alara.

"It is with great pleasure…"

One of the Queen's ladies chuckled and stared at Dono and some of the other ladies' cheeks turned pink as they bit their lips. Maraleine glared at them and continued.

"…that I honor our noble and brave Warriors for their acts of heroism. These Warriors have endured relentless training for years on end to ensure they are capable of both using their skills and strength to defend our people, *and* to control their emotions so as never to act in malice or unease. These heroes here tonight will be remembered in history as those who rose above. Those who fought for justice and succeeded. Indeed, while we have our mediators and our listeners who are often able to ensure our peoples remain peaceful, there are occasional times where the peace cannot be kept without force. It is in these rare cases we rely on these strong, brave souls to protect us all. Here's to the Warriors!"

With her goblet raised high, Queen Maraleine

gestured first to Dono, who smiled back with love in his eyes, and then toward the large table of fighters: now cleaned, gowned and relaxed on ale. Cheers rose up and the hall filled with the tinkles of silver spoons hitting crystal goblets...an almost magical sound.

Chapter 17 - Moving Forward (Now)

Emmeldine felt stuck. It was not a feeling she was familiar with. Never before had she felt such unease, such uncertainty. While her elite force continued to train in both basic battle skills and magic, she felt more and more like she could not be herself. She had to hide from Tharin and she had to hide from her court and people, lest she be "discovered' in her secrets. Her secrets now defined her.

Tharin, she could tell, was trying to be respectful of her boundaries. He was attentive, yet gave her needed space and was understanding of her distance. He did not push. Emmeldine was relieved by this; she had more urgent matters to attend to. Shaima and she had decided to test out their group of magic defenders by taking them to one of the villages that had reported "odd" events. Their theory was that these events might be related to magical creatures trying to enter this realm. Perhaps if this happened when the defenders were present, they could practice their skills. Perhaps they could even stop bad things from happening for good.

As they readied for departure, Tharin slowly approached her near the stables. Emmeldine looked up from the saddle bags she was adjusting, not trusting the normal stable hands to touch her unsanctioned cargo. She quickly stepped back as she saw a figure in turquoise approach (the color Tharin most often wore since Emmeldine said it suited him well). She suddenly smelled a rich scent of burnt wood and cinnamon, and she smiled at the comforting familiarity of his person. As he neared, his serious expression turned into a large smile, twinkling eyes crinkling kindly at her.

"I really wanted to wish you well before you depart. I fear our last conversation alarmed you, and it means an immense amount to me that you not head out without understanding me better."

As she opened her mouth to protest, Tharin's firm

arm reached up and gently put a finger on her pursed, pink lips. She quivered, heart beating faster, an odd mix of arousal and surprise. No one touched her without permission! Thinking of a calming technique Shaima taught her, she quickly followed her breath, picturing glowing light around them both. Tharin seemed to sense her calming and continued.

"Please, if you will let me finish. I need you to know the truth. I sense you fear I may be some sort of spy, or someone self-serving. This could not be further from the truth. I was brought to the castle as a young lad and worked in many a setting. I helped the baker, I assisted the groom, I gardened, I mended and I sewed. I did it all. My family was poor and my mother ailed at a young age. My father could not support me and my three brothers on his own, so was forced to put us into prosperous homes to get by. To me, this palace is home. I am good friends with most of the workers. I was liked by your mother and tolerated by your and Alara's fathers, I thought. And I watched you. I found you fascinating — I always have. I have wanted to befriend you for years, to discuss what's on your mind, to play and celebrate together. It was not until this recent season that I was brave enough to try. I am not a self-serving male, Emmeldine. In fact I am a male who lives to serve. The thing is, lately, I only wish to serve you."

With the last, he bowed deeply and then looked up with watery eyes and held out a shaky hand towards her. When she grasped it with her own smaller, warm one, his tense face broke into a smile as wide as a river. She pulled him near as his tantalizing scent of wood filled her nostrils. Turning her own grinning face up to his and slowly closing her eyes, she offered her plush lips to his eager attentions.

Later, as Emmeldine was riding furiously with her band of women, she thought back on her last moments with Tharin and the kiss they shared... and a pleasant heat permeated her body in a most desirable way.

They rode long and hard through countryside

Emmeldine had never seen during her sheltered life at court. She was awed by the beauty of various meadows flowering in wide rays of colors. Her eyes drank in dense forests that gayly glistened green in the sunlight and branches that hung heavily at sunset. Rivers and valleys abounded. On the third night, they were nearing their destination and decided to make camp early to avoid being spotted by the local folk...or something worse.

There were twenty of them in all, including trained Warriors and the newly formed group of magic users. Emmeldine was concerned about Shaima, who was obviously tiring more easily than the others. The elder woman was strong of spirit and heart and never complained, yet her pain was obvious from the winces and grimaces Emmeldine caught on her face when Shaima thought she was unobserved. Emmeldine requested extra stops and rest periods to help her old friend whenever she could. Other times, they were in unsuitable camping terrain near dusk and had to push on briskly to find shelter before the night enveloped them. Emmeldine noticed that Sarsha was keeping an eye on her old friend as well, and that warmed her heart.

Chloe pulled her chestnut mare up near Emmeldine and gestured toward the distant horizon. "There it be! Tis Dunanbar for sure!"

Emmeldine squinted and looked back at Chloe with a frown, "You mean that speck of clear land near the horizon?"

Chloe nods, "Yes indeed! It be but a small farming town, that be the first farm. I canna' wait to try our magics!"

Emmeldine nodded slowly and squinted back at the distant view. Luckily, it was still early day and they should have many hours to explore before the night cloaked any would-be aggressors.

"I forgot — you grew up in country near here, didn't you Chloe? That must have been so very different from our life at court."

"Aye indeed! I canna' say I have ever felt truly at home in the palace. A bit like a fish outta water you see? I am glad to be on familiar land, that be for sure!"

"I'm sure you are. Well, I do apologize we won't be going to your home lands specifically. Although, I suppose it's a good thing the disturbances do not seem to be near there."

"Aye! I am ever so glad, my Queen. Them wee beasties best stay away from my own. That pleases me greatly."

Perhaps not so wee, Emmeldine thought, praying to be wrong. As they neared the first signs of life — farmed lands — Emmeldine let her group of Warriors surround her. Insisting Shaima ride by her side, the older woman smiles at her reassuringly. They neared a small farm and saw a thin male on the porch looking out at them and a strong-looking thick woman striding in from the fields, headed right toward them.

As she got closer, the Warriors in front of the Queen spaced themselves just far enough apart so that she got a good view of the woman. Emmeldine saw a hardened face, skin thick with sun and brown hair coarse and dusty. The male on the porch behind her, presumably her mate, rose but did not move nor speak. Emmeldine thought it odd that there were no animals or children anywhere to be seen.

"We don't want no trouble here, we have no part in…" The woman stopped as she spotted Emmeldine's royal purple tunic in the group before her. Her eyes grew large as Emmeldine stepped forward gracefully.

"No part in what? Of what do you speak, good woman?"

"Oh, oh... your Majesty. I didn't realize it was you. Please, please tell me how I may be of service." The woman bowed her head and then glanced back at the male, shouting "Maredo, get some cool water for her Majesty at once! Don't dawdle!"

Maredo turned quickly into the house, disappearing

through its small entrance.

Emmeldine grimaced and quickly said, "That is not necessary. I appreciate your hospitality but please do not go to any trouble for us; we are just passing by. Although I would like to ask you a few questions, if I may?"

"Of course, your Majesty. Whatever can I do for you? I apologize we do not have much to offer. Maredo is a terrible homekeeper and I am forced to work the land by myself since he has also failed to give me any children. A pathetic male to be sure!"

Emmeldine stiffened and felt unpleasant heat rise in her chest, but considering the circumstances of their arrival, she tried to ignore this woman's obvious unkindness and verbal cruelty towards her mate.

"We are here to help. I have heard reports of unusual events and unease. Please, good woman, can you tell me what you yourself have heard or seen?"

The woman hesitated, her shoulders rising and her jaw stiffening. Her murky brown eyes shifted quickly from side to side. Emmeldine noticed a faint aura of anxiousness around the woman, an aspect of her new magic abilities that seemed to come and go randomly. The unease tasted and smelled like a bitter herb, and once again she struggled not to grimace.

"What is it? You need not fear us; we are here to help."

"And for that I am grateful, dear Queen. It has been a hard time here as of late. First the drought, then our animals started disappearing mysteriously, and then… Well, then, odd things started to be heard. And some say seen." She looked over to where Maredo had come back onto the porch, this time holding a glass container of water.

"I see. What type of odd things? Please, give me as much specific information as you can. I need to know."

"Well… There have been some odd lights yonder there." The woman points to the woods west of the house. "Also sounds. At night. First I thought them canines, beasts of the land, yet the sounds weren't quite right. My pathetic mate over there tried to act brave and offered to go outside and check. That's when he noticed all our fowl were gone — not a feather left! He ventured toward the wood and came racing back shortly, saying he saw glowing eyes in the dark that stared at him evilly. Course probably just a damn critter but that be what he said!"

The woman huffed and spittle blew out of her cheeks toward Emmeldine. Emmeldine tried to remain composed as she turned toward Maredo. Shaima, who had approached from Emmeldine's left side, glanced at Emmeldine for permission, and with her nod of approval, headed over to the porch to speak quietly with Maredo. Emmeldine looked back at the woman who was suspiciously watching the porch.

"Pardon me, dear woman — I have yet to acquire your name?'

"Oh! Well, your Majesty, I am humbled. I am the meager farmer Annetta. Please forgive my poor manners. We do not see many travelers out this way. Maredo is such a poor conversationalist that the only time I hear my own voice is to yell at him. 'Specially now that my animals are gone. I do miss them damn swine!"

Shaima walked back to the group and nodded, then turned toward the horses.

"Thank you, dear Annetta. We shall venture into the woods ourselves and promise to return any animals that may belong to you. Please tell Maredo not to worry, we have had success stopping rare creatures before. The Goddess is protecting us. Fare thee well." Emmeldine nodded her head and marched away quickly, struggling to keep a neutral expression on her face.

Daria approached her right side, a tight frown on her normally peaceful face. "That woman was abhorrent! How could you be so polite to her? She certainly doesn't deserve it!"

"No one has hate in their heart for no reason, dear

friend. Even angry, hateful Annetta deserves our compassion and respect."

"She's so unenlightened and ugly of soul. Is this how it is with country folk? I had heard tale but honestly, well, I thought most people think like us. That everyone deserves love and respect."

"This is as new to me it is to you Daria; we have both lived rather sheltered lives I fear."

"I am starting to see that. I wonder what else we shall learn on these journeys. I have a feeling there is much to come."

"Aye, for sure there is." Emmeldine's face fixed into a grimace as she strode briskly toward the woods.

Chapter 18 – New Life (Then)

Some time passed, and both Dono and Reynaldo stayed at court — an occurrence that was unfamiliar to all involved. There was an uneasy truce between the men vying for Maraleine's attentions. It was understood that Reynaldo shared her chambers at night, and that Dono was mostly there to spend time with his daughter and regain his strength after the physical ordeal he had undergone with the Warriors. Maraleine's health seemed to flourish under the attentions of her chosen mates and she exuded both health and power. Her skin was clear and rosy with a healthful glow, her voice musical and strong, and her body appeared thicker, as if she was finally eating enough to sustain it. You could almost hear the sigh of relief from both nobles and servants alike. Emmeldine was especially pleased.

After a private conversation with her mother, Emmeldine decided to seek Alara out. The sisters had spent little time together as of late; Emmeldine immersed in her studies and time with her father, and Alara supposedly doing the same. Emmeldine suspected that Alara had been avoiding her, though. It was subtle at first. Emmeldine noticed that Alara wasn't seeking her out and did not seem enthusiastic when her elder sister offered companionship. Then Alara outright snapped at Emmeldine several times and ran away from her — most unusual.

The sky was murky one day, clouds rolling past at a steady clip. Winds kicked up as Emmeldine searched the children's wing and then headed to the gardens. Seeing a flash of pale hair through the shrubbery, Emmeldine entered a small maze.

"Alara? Is that you? Come out here. I must speak with you."

She heard giggling and rustling as the wind picked up. Emmeldine followed the sounds and saw the blond head through cracks between the plants. She wasn't too far ahead.

Suddenly Emmeldine heard a voice and froze in her tracks.

"Patience… you must practice harder… keep from your father… tell no one."

The crackly aged voice jolted a sense of recognition in her, but she could not quite understand why. Then she saw a figure outside of the maze heading away from them. A torn grey cloak on a hunched figure. Surely that's not the Crone from the glen? How could she have gotten in here?

Emmeldine surged forward and found Alara heading toward her from the next row, long blond hair loose and blowing around her wildly.

"There you are! You come with me this instant!" With a shaking hand and flushed face, Emmeldine grabbed her little sister by the arm and pulled her out of the maze.

"What are you doing? Stop!" Alara started to cry.

"What are you doing out here? Whom were you speaking with?"

"Are you mad? I'm alone. Leave me be!" Alara pulled away and ran toward the palace with tears streaming down her cheeks.

Emmeldine sat down on a stone bench, face sunken, eyes squeezed shut. Her mind raced with questions. *What is going on here? Was that the Crone? Is she teaching Alara to use magic?* Emmeldine was so caught up in her thoughts that as she stood and slowly wandered into the castle, she failed to notice the wind had suddenly stopped the moment she touched Alara. All was still.

Emmeldine had originally sought out Alara to tell her some news she found rather important — news that she thought Alara deserved to know before all others. After their interaction in the maze, Emmeldine didn't see Alara anywhere… although she didn't look too hard. Confusion, worry, and an odd sense of dread stopped her. *This doesn't feel like what is meant to be, yet isn't everything always as it should be? How could it be anything else?* she wondered.

The next day, the Queen's ladies personally went around the castle to tell all family, nobles, and esteemed guests of the crown that the Queen was hosting a special meal that evening — and that she had an important announcement to make. Roast beasts would be served along with the normal decadent dishes of fresh produce in tantalizing sauces that the court regularly dined upon. Emmeldine saw Reynaldo several times talking in small groups, usually with other men — his eyes shimmering as he stood tall, looking very robust and strong. Almost like a proud bird displaying its plumage.

Emmeldine and Alara crossed paths leaving their wing, heading down the main hall toward the feasting chamber. Alara gave a small smile at her big sister and continued to amble toward the music and rumbling voices ahead. With a big smile, Emmeldine fell into step with her sister, shortening her pace to match hers companionably. Alara assumed her sister was as clueless as her to their mother's big announcement, so did not inquire. In truth, Emmeldine struggled with what to say, or whether to say anything at all. As they neared the gathering, Alara's eyes widened. Around the doorway before them were long thick wreaths of intricately woven flowers. Sweet, fresh scents intertwined and hit their noses all at once. So many varieties! There were beautiful couples heading arm in arm into the grand hall, dressed opulently in shimmering silks and embroidered fabrics from afar.

"Emmeldine, what is this about? This is a much bigger announcement than I had thought. The decor, the guests... something is happening, isn't it?"

Emmeldine noticed that her sister's previously whiny voice was beginning to sound more mature, like a young woman rather than a fussy child.

"Yes, dear Alara, it *is* a big thing, I suppose. You see…"

Before Emmeldine could finish, Alara turned away as her father, Dono, wandered up to them.

"Father!" She rushed into his arms, a large smile softening her previously furrowed brow. "Where have you been all day? I was searching for you!"

"I told you that I had to restart my physical training. I also met with specially trained Healers and a Priestess to ensure my aggression is in check and my feelings properly processed. It appears I am an enlightened male!" He laughed jovially and picked up his daughter to swing her around.

Alara laughed joyfully, "Of course you are, Father! You are most wonderful."

With a quick nod at Emmeldine, Dono quickly lowered Alara, tucking his arm through hers. They briskly strode into the hall, leaving Emmeldine alone.

A short time later, they were all seated in the feast room: Queen Maraleine at the high table with Alara and Dono to her right, and Emmeldine beside her father Reynaldo to her left. Shaima was nearby, and her mother's closest advisers sat just below. The entire chamber, which was quite large, was filled with well-dressed bodies beneath smiling faces. They looked up expectantly when a small gong was struck. The Queen rose.

"I thank you all for being here today. Today is a very joyous one for me and my husband king, Reynaldo."

She turned toward Reynaldo and he stood up and took her hand, smiling bashfully with a hint of pink touching his face. Still facing forward, she continued.

"I am very pleased to announce that I am carrying another female heir to Trimeria, the second in succession following our darling Emmeldine!"

Maraleine grasped her flowing gown and held it tautly against her burgeoning belly, a small firm mound protruding proudly. The room started to buzz with excited exclamations and cheers. Beaming, Maraleine raised their joined hands triumphantly and turned toward Emmeldine to grab her hand, too. The three of them, hands clasped, smiled and laughed — a small, happy family elated at their growing number. The gathered guests cheered triumphantly and clapped with gusto. Security and hope were being displayed for all to enjoy. So they did.

It was only when she sat down for the meal that Emmeldine thought to glance at Alara. Alara was staring at her mother and Reynaldo who were huddled together, whispering gaily. Alara's eyes were cold, her expression fluctuating from flat to grimacing to back again as she fought with her emotions. Dono was still beside her, not looking at anyone or anything. Emmeldine thought she saw a glimmer of wetness in his eyes but could not be sure. She quickly looked down at the plate being set before her and started to daintily cut up her roast beast. For reasons she couldn't quite place, she felt salty drops drip from her own face and quickly wiped them away. If anyone asked, she would tell them they were tears of joy.

Chapter 19 - The Woods (Now)

The Warriors do indeed find animals, and rather quickly... but they are not alive.

"Dear Goddess! Those look to be the carcasses of goats, fowl and swine scattered about that narrow trail over there." Sarsha and another Warrior quickly go to investigate while the others grimace in horror.

"No hoof prints or signs of other beings, My Queen." The Warrior gestured to the ground before her. "Only snatches of fur, feces and what I fear is the aftermath of ravenous feasting." Emmeldine held her breath as the stench hit her, face crinkling despite efforts to remain calm and not show her disgust. Emmeldine was very aware that while she was technically the leader of this group and they looked to her for strength and direction, she secretly relied on Shaima to direct her, still feeling very much a novice when it came to magic and the unknown.

They swiftly moved on. As the pungent smells faded she prayed quietly to the Goddess, "Please bless the creatures whose lives were taken. Protect my friends and I, dear Goddess — I worship thee." Up to this point, faith had been a given for Emmeldine — just something that was a part of her life and the lives of those around her, like breathing. Lately, however, Emmeldine felt a more personal relationship forming with the higher realm. She prayed regularly for strength and wisdom, but mostly she prayed for clarity. That when the time came, she would know what to do if confronted directly with her sister; that she would know how to handle her intensifying feelings for Tharin; and if she could navigate through all that, she prayed she would have the clarity to help her people accept magic. Her growing knowledge of magic illuminated that their world really was more mysterious than she had ever thought before, and there were apparently worlds she had never yet imagined. She often shivered at the thought. *What was out there?*

She thought back to her childhood as she often did of late, to a time she had attended worship with her mother. Maraleine was known to be a very devout Queen and took her role as the mouthpiece to the Goddess very seriously.

"Daughter! Do not dawdle, the Goddess waits for no one, not even a Queen."

"Forgive me Mother, I was distracted by the strange beauty."

Emmeldine rose from studying a spore she had noticed on a branch near their footpath. The royal pair had been taking in the fresh morning air as they made their daily stroll to the chapel of the Goddess. As they walked on, Emmeldine decided to ask her mother one of the many burning questions in her heart, those she rarely let escape.

"Mother, how do you know you are truly chosen by the Goddess? Does she speak to you?"

Emmeldine sensed her mother stiffen, but kept her face forward as she saw the glistening white marble walls beckoning to them.

"I know because I know, Emmeldine. I am the Queen. I was meant to rule. I was born knowing this, just as you were. I hope you will accept this sooner than later. For all our sakes."

"Yes Mother, yet the Goddess, how do you kn…."

"Enough! I shall not listen to such nonsense. I know. You shall know. Trust in me, Emmeldine. There is no one else who can know better than I. No one!"

"Yes, Mother. That must be true."

Her attention back on their current surroundings, Emmeldine realized they were now further into the woods and had come upon a slanted shack barely standing at all, if the rotted boards were any indication. They froze upon seeing it, aware that it was an ideal place for someone, or some*thing*, to be hiding with ill intent. Emmeldine had further reason to pause as she was transported back in time again — to shortly after her mother announced her last pregnancy.

She had been confused about how to talk with Alara and concerned about the odd incident in the gardens, so she decided to seek out the Crone and ask her directly if she was involved with her younger sister. The Crone's shack was easily found that day and did not take her by surprise. Emmeldine stomped up to it boldly, determined to get answers. As she approached, she smelled a dry, rotting stench and had to use the long sleeve of her travel tunic to cover her nose as she entered. The crunching sound immediately alerted her to the broken glass scattered all over the floor, which she luckily could not feel through her sturdy animal hide walking boots. The source of the stench was easily identified. Broken jars, various dead plants, rotten foods, and animal parts were strewn apart on the cracked floor, as if a small wind storm had torn through the shack like a flash. Emmeldine stifled a squeal as something ran across her toes. Her eyes followed its path to see a small brown rodent escape through the door she'd left open behind her.

"Is anyone here? … Please, respond thee now — it is I, Princess Emmeldine. … Hello?"

Nothing. Emmeldine thought to look around further but could no longer bear the stench as her eyes watered and her lungs started to strain. She quickly turned and gasped for fresh air as she passed back through the threshold to the brilliant sun beyond. Whatever had happened here, she felt very sure that the Crone was gone, never to return.

Back in the present, she shook her head to clear her mind of distressing thoughts. Emmeldine was confused about why the past was suddenly so forefront in her mind. It did not seem wise with possible danger nearby. She took a silent breath and looked to her left at her travel companions, giving a slight tilt of her head to the right to indicate her intentions.

With silent signals given by the lead Warrior, they started to move forward, slowly approaching the shack. It was near dusk in the dense woods. The air felt as if it were made of shadows, and all was still. Shaima gestured to the magic users indicating they should follow, and quickened her own pace to match the Queen's. Emmeldine started a low, murmured chant, barely audible to Chloe on her immediate right. She could see Shaima's lips moving in sync with hers from several yards away on the north side of the dwelling. They moved into place surrounding the shack from all angles, a white glow gently pulsing around them. The Warriors stood by and could not help but show surprise on their faces. Some jaws actually dropped as the glow brightened and shone. A shriek suddenly pierced the still air, and masses of birds rose from their hidden perches and ascended rapidly, squawking in protest. Soon, all was still. Emmeldine's heart pounded and her breath froze with anticipation. *What in the Goddess' name was that? Surely that sound was not of this world?* A sudden thump interrupted her thoughts, and she saw the side of the shack ripple. Shaima was gesturing emphatically and Emmeldine started to chant, the light glowing once again.

Crash! The south side of the shack fell, shattering to pieces. A large, furry limb thrust out, then another. A deep, rumbling growl was easily heard above her chant, although she had intensified her voice and Shaima's had also joined her. A couple of arrows arched overhead and landed near the broken wall, but Emmeldine furiously gestured for the Warriors to stop. The last thing she wanted was another dead magical being. She wanted *answers.* The growling continued, and she heard a scraping sound from within. As she and the magic users edged closer, she saw two glowing eyes within — a deep, burning amber. She reminded herself of what she and Shaima had discussed before embarking on this trip: that they needed a creature alive, hopefully something they could learn from somehow, although communication would be tricky at best. Remembering the spell for stunning a large body, she edged closer yet.

"*Mel ta doray mora, theyma trian bordu!*"

The growling intensified. Suddenly a very large creature — about double the size of the largest wolf in their realm — jumped straight at Emmeldine, fangs bared and claws extended. All at once, the magic users made physical contact with one another as Emmeldine finished the words she needed to stop the beast.

"Forsay mlacken dar!" The white light pulsed out directly at the beast and it fell from mid-air before them, one claw scraping the toe of Emmeldine's boot. Gasping, she hastily stepped back, and several of her band grabbed onto her for support. Her entire body began to tremble, and they helped her sit down a few yards back from the brown body. Shaima drew up to it and turned to nod back at the Queen that the creature was indeed subdued, but alive. Emmeldine smiled faintly in response. Her body shook slightly as her heart filled with warmth.

She knew a lot still needed to be done to secure the beast and find shelter for the night, but Emmeldine was not ready to do so. She needed some time to just *be*. Luckily, the Warriors were ready for action and eager to be a part of this mysterious event. They set up camp nearby and helped tie up the beast, who still appeared to be in deep slumber. Emmeldine tried not to think about what would happen when it woke. She prayed she had some time to rest and plan.

Chapter 20 - Life Went On (Then)

While Emmeldine was disturbed by the Crone's disappearance, she did not feel she had anyone to discuss the matter with. In the meantime, she decided to work on reaching out to Alara while avoiding interrogating her or putting her on edge in any way. Reynaldo was less available now that he was back in high favor with the Queen; everyone wanted some of his attention and time. He was the male who brought calm to the realm, who had given the Queen a second heir. Security. Several days after her venture into the woods, Emmeldine was able to search for Alara after her daily lessons were complete — a time she would usually use to walk with her father.

After inquiring with various servants, Emmeldine was directed toward the stables. According to the kitchen lad, it seemed her sister had a newfound love of horses. As she approached, Emmeldine heard a beautiful voice singing softly and peeked in a window to seek the source without alarming anyone within. Alara sat on her knees, left arm extended out toward a chestnut mare, fingers gently stroking the shiny fur back and forth. Emmeldine did not recognize the song but the tones were soft and sweet, like one would sing to a young babe. Comforting.

Alara went on to groom the mare while her sister secretly watched. Emmeldine, now nearly a grown woman herself, saw a flash of the adult her sister would soon become. Never before had she seen Alara so poised and confident. Emmeldine shifted a little and accidentally knocked over an empty barrel outside the window. The sound startled the horse, who shifted its body and snorted, causing Alara to look up. The look of anger in her green eyes flashed like vicious lightning toward the window as she spotted her sister. Emmeldine quickly rushed around the building to enter the stables and found her sister soothing the gentle giant before her.

"Alara, I am very sorry. I was mesmerized by your beautiful singing and accidentally knocked a barrel over. I hope your friend wasn't too disturbed."

"Oh, so it's my fault, is it? MY singing made you clumsy? Always something wrong with me and you, so perfect and divine?"

"What? No, Alara! That is not at all what ..."

Before Emmeldine could finish, Alara turned and bolted out of the stables. Her previously beautiful voice was now ugly sobs fading away as she ran. Stunned, Emmeldine stood still, her mouth slightly agape. Finally, she forced herself to put one foot in front of the other and slowly shuffled into the cool air outside. She never noticed the young male on the other side of the stables watching her with interest.

Alara continued to avoid Emmeldine, and the elder sister decided to give her some time. The poor girl had a lot to contend with emotionally, and Emmeldine thought it best to focus on the positive relationships around her. Maraleine was glowing with health and new life as her small rounded belly grew to resemble a sizable melon. The Queen seemed more and more interested in spending time with her eldest daughter, and the two were often seen strolling the gardens hand in hand. On one such day, Emmeldine decided to revisit her ownership of the wood beads, as it had been weighing on her heart since they entered her possession. They were sitting on a bench surrounded by stargazers, a tall yellow flower with long, peaked petals. The air was cool and the blue sky clear as was common for the late season in Trimeria. Emmeldine knew she was nearing the age of reason. Soon she would be allowed to rule the land should the need arise. She felt confident that her mother was young yet and that the time for Emmeldine to rule was far in the future.

"Mother, please let me give you the beads back. I want you to have them for the birth. Please hold them while you bring my sister into this world. It would comfort me to know you have their strength, and honestly... I am not ready for them. They should be with you."

"My dear, I did not know this was weighing on you so heavily. My mother handed them to me long before her time here was over and she told me to hand them to my first born daughter when I felt the time was right. So I did. You know I do not like to be questioned. I expect obedience from my children." Maraleine sniffed and gestured toward the beads Emmeldine held with a bemused grin. "Still, you will be Queen someday, and it is good you know your mind. With that said, I will not take them back for good, but I will hold them during my pains. I will hold them for strength and to be connected to both my foremothers and to you, my heart."

Maraleine reached out a hand to tenderly touch Emmeldine's cheek, and Emmeldine felt her eyes sting as several teardrops hit her rich, green velvet gown.

"You've never called me that before." she said quietly, wiping her eyes and looking up into her mother's own watery ones.

"You *are* my heart, child of mine. You are my legacy. And I know you will not disappoint me." With that, Maraleine pushed off the bench and awkwardly stood up, grabbing her lower back till she found her stride. "Come, let's get back inside before the chill sets in."

Emmeldine knew her mother must have felt uncomfortable being so emotional around her, for their region of Trimeria never got cold enough to chill. She had heard of frost and snow, but had yet to feel their cool touch. She wondered if her brothers living to the West had ever known snow. She shook the thought away. It always saddened her to think of the brothers she barely knew.

Chapter 21 - Once Again (Now)

The beast slumbered for what felt both like never ending purgatory and the blink of an eye. After trying to nap in her tent, Emmeldine sought out Shaima to discuss the creature and make a plan for when it woke. Shaima was sitting on a fallen tree about a hundred feet from the tied-up creature. A foul smell similar to that of the first creature they'd encountered hugged the air tightly. Emmeldine crinkled her nose and sat down beside her friend.

"Well then… another beast found. What say you, Shaima? Is this a creature from another realm, sent by my sister? Or merely a wolf of the likes we have never seen?"

As she finished speaking, the creature let out a soft growl and extended its front claws, yet its eyes remained closed. *Do beasts dream?*

"I am certain this is a magical creature. Nothing of our realm can move like that. Its shape and size alone are quite unusual. Yes, it does closely resemble a wolf, yet it has some different features. For one, I thought I saw a double row of teeth when it snarled, but I dare say I am not willing to get close enough to its jaw to find out just yet. Its body is too large and moves too differently to simply call it Canine. I am thinking we should do a containment spell to keep it still, then wake it. I would very much like to know if it can speak, and if so, what it may wish to say."

The other magic users had quietly moved up behind them as Shaima spoke, and Emmeldine felt Daria's firm hand on her shoulder. She looked up to see her friend's serious face change to a small smile, a nod of her head. They were ready.

Shaima started chanting softly, then the other women joined in. Emmeldine focused her energy on their words and felt a warmth tingle on her skin. The soft white glow she was starting to expect radiated softly outward. Shaima continued to chant, joining hands with Emmeldine to point the light at the slumbering beast. White light formed around it and became more solid, making the beast appear like an object in a painting, the glow its canvas. The voices faded, then stilled, yet the glow continued.

The Warriors came in closer to the group, weapons ready, all eyes set on the same furry heap. Shaima nodded at Emmeldine. The Queen took a deep breath, stood a little taller, and raised a hand toward the beast. Its eyes snapped open.

Chapter 22 - Bringing Life (Then)

When an ordinary woman in Trimeria is about to give birth, her female relatives and nearby friends gather at her home. They cook hearty foods and surround the mother-to-be with her favorite scents and flowers, caring for her as elaborately as possible. When a Queen is about to give birth, however, she must select her company carefully. It is one of the highest honors in the land to attend the Queen during her labors and to see firsthand her bring a being chosen by the Goddess into this realm. Emmeldine and Shaima were to be there that day. Alara was not. Emmeldine tried to encourage her mother to add Alara to the list but she wouldn't budge, claiming only those with special purpose should attend. A few of Reynaldo's female relatives were invited, and several additional Priestesses and Healers. True to her promise, Maraleine held the sacred wooden beads as her pains started to take her breath away.

"I'm here, Mother. You are bringing me another sister. She is loved. You are doing wonderfully."

Emmeldine looked down at the beads clasped between her mother's hands and noticed how polished and worn they were, full of energy. They almost seemed to shine.

Both Emmeldine and Shaima encouraged the Queen and performed little gestures of care for her. They would wipe her brow and hand her a cup of oxtail broth to sip, but mostly they sat back and let the divine happen. Maraleine was looking rather strained and pale, her responsiveness lagging. It became time to push and she squatted with a woman on each side of her, holding their arms for support.

"AAAAAAaaaaaa... GODDESS HELP ME....."

She screamed, panted, grunted and wept. Day turned to night, which then turned to dawn. After breaking to rest for a while, the now-weakened Queen rose with assistance and gave a hard stare into Shaima's eyes. Shaima gave a slight nod and grasped the Queen's hands, beads around them both. They whispered a blessing together and Emmeldine joined in, worried for her mother. Maraleine pushed with all her might, and a light-haired head started to emerge from between her quivering thighs. Their voices joined again and rose in intensity. Emmeldine thought she saw a spark of white light between her mother's legs but knew she must be nearing exhaustion herself. With a final wail, Maraleine pushed with all her might and a slippery little creature slid from her womb into the waiting hands of its big sister.

A rush of love the likes of nothing she had ever imagined cascaded through her as the infant looked up with dark eyes smudged with birth matter. Wiping the baby's eyes, she then cleared her mouth and ears, looking her over as she'd been taught. Every girl in Trimeria learns to attend births from a young age: it's a valued part of the sacred feminine. The babe was definitely a girl as foretold, though a small one. And there was something about the look of her that didn't seem... *right*. Emmeldine reluctantly handed her off to one of the Healers to attend to and noticed her mother had been lifted onto the bed, her eyes shut. Slow, raspy breaths came from her pale lips and Shaima was by her side, holding her hand yet again.

"What is wrong? Mother?" Emmeldine hurried to her side and took her other hand. She barely registered the Healer attending to the afterbirth and clearing her mother's sacred channel. She looked to Shaima.

"What is happening? Is she well?"

"It was a very difficult birth, Emmeldine. Your mother is not well. We are doing what we can to help. The rest is up to the Goddess."

Shaima's face appeared more wrinkled and worn than Emmeldine had ever noticed before. Dark circles hung beneath her eyes and her skin was an ashy gray. She continued staring down at the Queen while she spoke, then looked up into Emmeldine's hopeful eyes. Her own eyes shone with tears.

Finally, her mother slept, and Emmeldine felt it was time to become acquainted with her new baby sister. She moved over to where the nursemaid was holding her: a tiny bundle indeed. Emmeldine gently folded back the blanket near her face and gazed at her sleeping form. There was definitely something about the shape of her face. Something was... *different*. The nurse gave her a half-hearted smile when she looked up, and that alarmed Emmeldine the most. *What was wrong with her baby sister?*

The day wore on and Queen Maraleine did not seem to improve. When she did regain some clarity, she requested to see Alara immediately. Reynaldo and Dono had both been sent off to separate country estates to allow space for the sacred feminine to bring forth new life, so they were not nearby.

"Shall we send for Father? Dono?" Emmeldine asked in a voice so tiny, she could barely hear herself.

Maraleine merely shook her head. Shaima put a hand on Emmeldine's shoulder and walked her to the door.

"I think it best that you prepare Alara for seeing your mother in this condition. She needs to understand that this may be goodbye."

Emmeldine started sobbing. Hearing the words she had feared the most was shocking to her soul.

"I....I..I don't know if I can."

"You can do this, my dear. You must. Your sister needs you."

With a weak nod of her head, Emmeldine turned toward the hall from which her sister would most likely enter, slowly putting one foot in front of the other.

She looked in all the places inside the palace that she thought Alara would be, but no sign of her. A handsome young male Emmeldine recognized as a prior serving lad informed her that he spotted Princess Alara heading to the stables earlier that day. He spoke with such kindness, and the concern emanating from his intense brown eyes made Emmeldine wonder if he knew their mother might die.

Heading in the direction he had indicated, Emmeldine was hesitant to disturb her sister in the stables once again... but she had no choice. She must bring her to Mother.

As she approached the stables, she once again heard a beautiful voice floating out of the open windows. A strong sense of déjà vu struck Emmeldine like a stone, and she tried frantically to think of how to make this interaction with Alara go better than the one before. She decided to enter from the main doorway, thus hopefully alerting her sister to her approach in a non-alarming manner. As she neared the entryway, she softly called out.

"Alara? Are you here? Alara?"

She heard shuffling and a small horse snort, but nothing else. She stepped in and saw the same chestnut mare at the back of the building... but no Alara. Suddenly, Alara stepped out of the shadows to the side of her mare, blond hair flowing behind her. She was dressed in earth toned riding gear, a sack at her side. Emmeldine was struck by the quiet heat between them and found it odd that the strong smell of hay smacked her senses so heavily.

"Well here we are again, sister. Come to scare my horse again, have you? You needn't bother — I am leaving. You have won. I am tired of being ignored, uninvited, not a "real" daughter. Tell Mother I am choosing to live with my father elsewhere. I wish her well with her new heir."

Her voice that had started out strong turned to sobs and she grabbed the horse's tether and started to pull her forward. Emmeldine stepped forward to block her path.

"Alara! What are you saying? This is madness! Mother isn't well. You *can't* go! And the baby... the baby has come and... she doesn't seem right."

Alara tried to push past Emmeldine, her horse at her side.

"Alara, STOP!"

A flash of golden light shot from Emmeldine's fingers as she raised her hand toward Alara's shoulder, and Alara shrieked as she raised her hand to block. The light hit the mare instead and she crumpled to the ground like a leaf. Alara screamed and pulled herself away from the falling creature just in time to avoid being crushed under its weight. She cried in loud gasps, her eyes flashing at her sister with a coldness so raw that Emmeldine wasn't sure she could breathe. Somehow air continued to enter her lungs.

"YOU KILLED MY HORSE!" A fierce wind started to whip around them, hair and clothes swaying.

"Alara, I... I don't know what happened, it was an acc.."

"YOU KILLED MY ONLY FRIEND! YOU DID THIS!"

The wind intensified and pushed Alara forward, even as it held Emmeldine in place.

Sobbing, Alara turned away, grabbed her travel gear and ran out the stable doors. Emmeldine, speechless, sunk to the ground. After she stilled her heart with some slow breaths, she thought to look at the horse's neck and saw a faint pulse beating. She noticed a shimmering green light around the fallen equine. It was alive.

Chapter 23 - Moving On (Now)

Amber glowing eyes looked straight into hers, and Emmeldine felt her soul quiver. The creatures eyes seemed to change color randomly. *Was this evil?* The Goddess taught of fighting hate with love, of doing right instead of wrong. This creature felt very, *very* wrong. Emmeldine raised a arm out, palm up, as a gesture of goodwill. The creature snarled and tried to lunge toward her but its bonds, both physical and magical, restrained it. Taking a step back, Emmeldine looked at the group behind her for support. Marianee stepped forward and whispered in her ear. Emmeldine nodded, so Marianee approached the creature. The beast was still now. It seemed to understand it was trapped and that it was no use to strain itself. Marianee eyed the gnarly beast silently, assessing its features, showing no reaction when her eyes examined the long claws or protruding fangs.

"Do you have a message for us? Tell us, why are you here?"

Silence.

"Did Alara send you?"

The creatures now green eyes grew larger and a low rumble thundered from its chest and up its throat in a predatory growl. Yet, no decipherable reply. Marianee continued to stare it down, her shoulders stiff and fists clenched.

Suddenly there was a crackle from the direction of the shack and white light spilled out of the woods around it. Emmeldine and Shaima took off toward it, yelling at the others to stay put and keep the beast contained. As they reached within a hundred feet of the shack, the rumbling stopped and a single blue glowing orb shot out. *A Fairy!*

Emmeldine and Shaima both gasped for air with eyes open wide as they suddenly stopped sprinting. The Fairy flew within five feet of them and started to pulse a faint purple. The lilac orb grew larger, and Emmeldine realized the Fairy itself was growing. The orb continued to expand until she was as big as a human. Her body was long and narrow, her viridescent skin radiated life like a young fern. Where hair should have been on her head was a smooth cap of darker skin, almost black. Her wings shimmered at first, then an almost translucent blue folded back and disappeared from view. The light faded, and the Fairy blinked her dark purple, slanted eyes and breathed a slow breath through lips as pink as a kitten's nose. And then, much to both women's delight, she spoke.

"You are in great danger."

Her voice was musical, almost as if the notes of a song were being translated into words they could understand.

"Your sister Alara is trying with all her might to send magical creatures to harm you; she intends to take over the realm. Right now they are testing entry points and your defenses, gathering information for her. As you can see, this is now an entry point. I can teach you how to barricade it from magic users, but there will be others."

Both Emmeldine and Shaima opened their mouths to respond, but the older woman spoke first.

"We thank the Goddess for sending you. You are a beacon of hope. Please, can you tell us if others are coming to help? Shall we prepare for a battle?"

The dark orbs fixed on Shaima, never blinking during the long silence. Finally her tiny mouth opened and her musical voice flowed outward like a gentle river, "I cannot stay long, it is challenging for me to stay in this form and you will not be able to understand my communication if I am in my natural state. I will tell you speedily – yes, more are coming, and there could be a battle. Prepare. We will send our brethren when we see fit. It is not viable for our people to remain in your realm long or often, so we must be wise. In the meantime, you must block any entry points you can find. Look for the lights, for unusual happenings — that is where you will find them."

The ethereal being turned her elegant head toward

the hairy beast, showing no expression.

"This thing will not help you. It cannot speak your language and has been poisoned against you to hate. Regretfully, you must end its life."

Emmeldine opens her mouth to speak but was silenced by a spectacular sight before her. The Fairy started to shrink, her green and purple form fading in both color and size. As she neared the size of a teapot, her wings folded out and she began to hover. She continued to shrink until at last, she was the size of a teacup. The Fairy flew up to Emmeldine's face and looked her purposefully in the eyes. With a slight nod of her head, she turned and flew away toward the shed, darting into what remained of the structure and disappearing from their lives.

"I didn't even get her name," she sighed.

"Worse yet, she did not teach us how to barricade the entry." Marianee briskly responded.

Luckily, as the women examined the shack, they were fairly confident the entry point had indeed sealed when the Fairy left. The lights were completely extinguished and there were no unpleasant smells, sounds, or any other indications of magic present. All was still. Chloe darted out, then in again, smiling widely.

"The forest sounds are back! It was silent around this part when we captured the beastie. Now, them birds are chirpin'!"

Emmeldine smiled in relief. They were safe — at least for now.

Chapter 24 - When Things Move Too Fast (Then)

After pausing for some deep breaths, Emmeldine wiped the stinging liquid from her eyes, brushed herself off, and set out to find her sister. She had to tell her the horse was alive — merely stunned, it seemed. Emmeldine started to shake whenever she thought about the white light, so she found a dark corner of her mind and tried to store those thoughts away. As she frantically headed to the main entry to the palace, she saw several people rush out the door straight toward her. She didn't have time to register who they were before their voices struck her like cold lightning.

"Emmeldine! Come quick! Hurry!"

She raced forward.

"What has happened? Is Mother okay? The baby?"

The lady and Emmeldine's aunt, Reynaldo's sister Claraceit, looked at her with silent, soulful eyes. Finally, after Emmeldine thought her heart must have stopped beating moons ago, Claraceit cleared her throat and softly uttered, "It is your dear Mother, Ordained Ruler, blessed by the Goddess. She is flickering, my love — her candle about to go out. Dear Emmeldine, you must get upstairs hastily, before it's too late."

Before her aunt could finish her sentence, Emmeldine took off running up the stairs, tears streaming down her cheeks, mind blank but for the thought of reaching her mother. Thinking was dangerous. She ran past the guards outside her mother's chambers, not noticing the fresh wreaths of flowers hung everywhere to welcome her baby sister, nor the ladies waiting outside with worried faces and tear cloths wringing. Emmeldine loudly pushed open the inner chamber doors and nearly slid into her mother's bedside. She grabbed Maraleine's hand, which were still clasping the wooden beads. Swiftly, Emmeldine wrapped the beads around their two hands, uniting them as they had been at her own birth.

"I am here Mother, I am here." The dripping tears became a waterfall as the dam controlling her emotions burst. She was grief-stricken over her mother, angry and worried about Alara, and fearful of having done harm to the equine creature below in the stables. The cacophony of thoughts cleared as she looked down at the pale person that now merely resembled her mother — a barely familiar face now sallow and lifeless. Maraleine's chest faintly moved up and down, raspy sounds rattling from her lungs at irregular intervals. Shaima put a hand on Emmeldine's shoulder and rubbed it softly.

"My dear Emmeldine, your mother is about to leave this realm. This is the time to say goodbye. Did you find Alara?" Her voice dropped to barely a whisper at the last.

Emmeldine couldn't move her head, her whole body was cold and she barely managed not to shake. Lying was unthinkable, yet even worse was the truth. She chose silence. She stayed kneeling near her mother till the end, hands bound by the beads, tears slowly and silently falling from her mother's pale, spectre-like face. Her aunt and several of the ladies tried to offer solace, tea, broth. Emmeldine responded with the faintest nudge of her head side to side and silence. They understood. When the end came, Maraleine let out a soft musical sound like nothing Emmeldine had ever heard before. A faint, golden light glowed for one quick moment around their joined hands, then she was gone — and the light gone with her. Emmeldine blinked furiously and then froze completely. Silence hung heavily.

She fought her brain so hard not to think. Not to think of Alara missing saying goodbye to their mother; not to think of their baby sister, still unnamed, who would never know her mother; not to think of the horse she nearly killed; not to think of which events were or were not her fault; and of course... magic. No, she mustn't think of that. Mother had warned her.

Near catatonia, she finally thought clearly enough to

realize there had been no baby sounds for some time and thought to ask for her sister. Claraceit looked at her sternly. Her features, normally a softer version of Reynaldo's, now looked cold and hardened.

"The baby is unwell. Something has been wrong with it since birth. My travel companion and a nursemaid are preparing to leave with me to take the baby back to my homelands where there are Healers and Priestesses familiar with such issues. Do not concern yourself with her — you have much you will need to attend to. I will take the best care of the child that is possible now." Relieved the baby was still alive, Emmeldine could only nod. Claraceit took this as consent and exited hurriedly out of the room, holding a wrapped bundle closely to her chest.

Daria showed up then, and gently putting an arm around the princess' petite shoulders, led her back to her own chambers to rest. Emmeldine had never felt so alone.

Chapter 25 - Too many Points (Now)

The canine beast was meant to be buried in the woods, but it dissolved to ashes before the hole could be dug. The group headed home. The band of magic users and Warriors were about a half day's ride from the palace when several of the Queen's spies intercepted them in a flowery glen. A tall blond spy named Freena bowed her head and put her small fingers together beneath her chin as it rose, and the shorter, darker woman named Eunica gave a downcast nod of her head and kept her eyes lowered as she spoke.

"My Queen, Freena and I crossed paths as we both raced toward you. There are strange occurrences to the North and the South. We both have had many reports of strange lights, unpleasant smells that are unfamiliar and foul, and sounds that still the heart. So far, these are from women who were away from their homes foraging, hunting, or pleasure riding. As of several moons ago, when we both headed to find you, no people had been harmed. There were a few reports of animals torn apart, but I am not certain those are related."

Emmeldine's piercing blue eyes widened and she turned to Shaima, a determined look upon her face.

"We must split up then, mustn't we? We have to stop them. But how then can we learn to block these ports of entry? Can we recall the Fairies?"

The last was said in a whisper as she leaned toward her shrunken friend. Shaima looked up at her with weary, drooping eyes and nodded. She gestured for the Queen to come away from the others for a private conversation.

"I think I have what I need with me to summon again: I brought the box. Unfortunately, I think we must split up. I hate to divide us up and weaken us in any way, but I don't see a way around it. Emmeldine… I hate to bring this up now, but it is a desperate time… "

Shaima paused and looked at her Queen, her friend.

With pained eyes, she slowly took a deep breath.

"Yes? What is it, Shaima? You can say anything to me, surely we have learned that about one another by now?"

Shaima quietly nodded and slowly opened her mouth to speak.

"It has occurred to me that magic runs deep in your family — even Alara may have the use of it or at least knows how to attain it. We are about to be divided in half. Who knows how many more times divisions will occur? We need more help. It has long been rumored that your baby sister did indeed live, that she is out there and well. Perhaps she can access magic — perhaps *she* can help us?"

Emmeldine froze, her mouth agape, her eyes widening and then narrowing.

"WHAT?! I have NEVER heard this. I would have searched the realm for her, I would have scoured the lands! I..."

Emmeldine suddenly found standing quite challenging and sat upon the nearest tree stump. She lowered her head and held it with her trembling hands, her red hair hanging in front of her face and gleaming like rubies. Everyone in the group had long ago backed off, sensing the two women, the leaders of their group, needed privacy to plan. Away from the others, the air was quiet between them for a few moments except for some cheery bird calls and rustling leaves as a soft breeze occasionally blew by. Finally, Emmeldine looked up with a flushed face and stared at her friend. Shaima began to speak in a soft, shaky voice.

"I know. I know you would have. I had many reasons not to mention this to you. All of which seem invalid to me now, but somehow very important back then. I hope you can trust me when I say — I did what I thought was right. You had been through so much: losing your mother, Alara's disappearance, having to prepare for coronation while the whole court was in chaos. Reynaldo and Dono all but abandoned you... I just — I didn't think you needed another thing to keep you up at night, to make your heart weary. I wanted to protect you. You should know, when magic users who are united by blood work together, their magic is more powerful. Your sister would be but a young girl; yet joining her power with yours might be powerful indeed."

With a big sigh, Emmeldine stood up and took Shaima's hand. She looked down at it: the blue veins near the surface so hard, the skin so soft and thin. *Time takes us all so quickly. I mustn't waste anymore time.* She rubbed her friend's hand thoughtfully for a moment, then looked up and smiled, her whole face lit up from within and blue-hazed love flowing out toward her companion.

"Tell me everything you know."

Several hours later, the group divided into two. Marianee and Sarsha would head north with Shaima, and Daria and Chloe would go south with Emmeldine. Five Warriors would accompany each grouping while the rest would return to the palace to ensure protective measures would be taken there. They felt the need to make haste and get to their destinations quickly, but Shaima assured the Queen that she would summon the Fairies that evening while her team set up camp. Or at least, she would try to.

They rode hard, Emmeldine focusing intensely on her stallion and the path before them. She thought of what she could do to magically subdue whatever they were heading toward: she practiced prayers, chants, and spells in her head. She did everything she could to prepare, and to not think about her sisters.

The next day they neared the town of Asdagray, the nearest settlement to the alleged happenings in the South. It was a good-sized town, prospering with trade and commerce. Emmeldine eyed the shop fronts and vendor stands as her band unsuccessfully tried to enter town quietly. The magic users and Warriors entered the first open storefront once they realized how much attention was being paid to them, lest the Queen be recognized. Emmeldine had drawn her riding cloak around her despite the pleasant weather, and kept the hood up as they entered what appeared to be a pleasant ale house. Several women reclined on stools near the barrel desk, and a bored-looking lad lazily wiped at spots on the tables. At the far end, a robust, scantily clad woman with a smile that did not seem to move looked up at them and motioned to a table in the corner. They quickly went to it and sat down.

"You all get cozy now ya ken? I'll be right with you ladies, and yer gents too I suppose."

She nodded to the lad, and he quickly grabbed some mugs and started filling them with ale. The woman grabbed the first four when full and hurried to them, her eyes flat and her wide smile thinning to a friendly smirk. Plunking the mugs on the wooden slab before them, she quickly motioned for the lad behind her to wipe up the spills, which he did swiftly after setting down the other mugs.

"We don't usually allow males in here. Don't want no trouble. In my experience men can't handle their drink. But I ken tell ya been traveling from afar, so I will let you be this one time."

Emmeldine let Marianee speak for them, lest her identity be compromised.

"Thank you good woman, we appreciate your hospitality. You need not worry about our friends here, they are good males, highly trained, and we are prepared to compensate you grandly for your leniency. As well as any information you can provide."

Chloe pulled out a plump coin purse, and the Tavern mistress' mouth fell open before the big loose smile returned to her face.

"I'll tell ya anything I can, lassie! Just you ask away!"

"Thank you, kind woman — we appreciate your generosity." Marianee gave a slight bow of her head.

Emmeldine stifled a laugh. The Mistress' head snapped to look at her, eyes narrowing, before dismissing her as nobody of import and looked back to Marianee.

"We would like to know about rumors of lights,

sounds, possible mysteries from the wild near here. Have you heard of such things?"

The woman frowned and pulled up a stool, easing her large backside onto it deftly.

"Aye, yes, there have been such things said. When they was said in here I must admit I paid no mind. Many an unusual conversation is heard when ale is abound. But then, well, I have most recently been hearing things when I'm in the market, no ale to be seen. Strange smells in the countryside, unexplained glowing lights at night, sounds...strange sounds that turn yer skin cold 'n ya heart to ashes. That's what they be sayin'."

"Where exactly are these things heard or seen...or smelled?"

The Mistress opened her mouth and then hesitated, so Marianee added, "We are here to help — we are beast hunters of sorts, and we stopped another similar event north of Briarwood. We can help here too, if you tell us all you know." She placed her fingers together and bowed her head deftly. The Mistress appeared surprised by the formal sign of respect, happily so. Her big smile returned and Emmeldine noticed there were several large gaps in her mouth where teeth should have been. The Mistress sat up taller and pushed out her ample bosom, then started to speak.

"Oh yes, I do recall some talk of such!"

After talking with the Mistress and resting for a while, the group reconvened outside the town. Emmeldine and Marianee whispered fervently to each other, then after reaching agreement, went over to their peers.

"We will go to the central point the barmaid told us about first, then if needed, we can look at the other possible sites. Chloe and I will use containment magic while you Warriors stand by weapons ready in case we can't hold it… them… whatever we come across. Understood?"

Daria cringed at the bossy tone of her royal friend and all but bit her tongue not to correct her about the Mistress' title and rank. This was not the time. Knowing her so well, she guessed the strain of the travel and the possibility of aggression were wearing her down.

They headed to a stream that had a rocky cove off one of its shores. Several picnickers and day trippers had noticed strange occurrences near there and it seemed to be at the center of all the reported events. As they neared, the sulfurous scent hit their noses like a bad dream and they winced before grabbing any sleeves or extra fabric they could find to block the stench. Emmeldine felt her body tightening as her hands grasped the bridle fiercely, her jaw clenching. She feared she couldn't contain it. And even if she could, how would they close the entryway?

By this time it was near nightfall; the bird calls were gone, the air was still. Nothing but the fading light from the sky and the quietly rippling waters assails their senses... and of course, the stench. They dismounted their horses and two of the Warriors led them away lest they get spooked. Emmeldine and the other magic users took a moment to center themselves, clear their heads, and wait. As the sky faded another shade and the gloom became inevitable, they saw the first sign. Bright red light shot up from a rocky outcropping on the far side of the stream a few yards down. They briskly jogged toward it, the Warriors in their group following close behind.

Emmeldine, Daria, and Chloe conversed quietly, deciding to band together to cast a containment spell.

"I'm worried we won't be able to connect together without Shaima — she has always united us." Emmeldine frowned.

Chloe looked at her with clear, shimmering eyes, a tender brightness shining from within. "We will. Do not worry now, we will." She grinned brightly and raised her hands palms up toward the lights.

Emmeldine sighed silently to herself and took a deep breath. She thought of Shaima, raised her hands, and started to chant. To her right, Daria joined her and soon the three of them were in unison, soft voices rising. The white glow

Emmeldine was beginning to expect rose up in front of them near the glowing rocks. Her chest tingled with pleasure. They finished the process and slowly lowered their hands, voices fading. The white light faded a bit but continued to glow around the eerie rocks, pulsing peacefully. After waiting some time for any sort of reaction, the women decided to rest in shifts. The sky was now inky dark around them and the majority of the group lay down on their mats and fell asleep.

"Thank you, Laniea, for volunteering to keep watch with me. I feel a bit more comfortable knowing I have a true Warrior by my side."

"My pleasure, my Queen; my life is to serve. If you want to rest, I promise to wake you at the slightest disturbance." Laniea bent her dark-haired head in respect, then looked directly into Emmeldine's eyes as if to show her how sincere she was. Her eyes burned with smoky brown intensity.

Emmeldine, not responding, slowly lay back and eventually closed her eyes. What felt like moments later, she heard a faint voice as if whispering from a great distance: "Sister, I am here. Emmeldine..." Emmeldine's eyes snapped open and she bolted upright, heart racing. *Alara is here!* Laniea was a number of strands away and rushed right to her despite the dark obscuring the land between them. She maneuvered the unseen terrain masterfully.

"Are you harmed?"

"No, no. A voice, I heard a voice. Over there!" Emmeldine whispered fervently and pointed toward the glowing rocks. *How can Alara be in there?*

"I heard not a thing, my Queen. Are you certain? A dream perhaps?"

Emmeldine shook her head, eyes fixed on the rocks. "No, I'm certain. I want to go in there and look. The spell is designed to keep others out, not us in — so we can safely permeate the shield."

"My Queen, please, allow me. I cannot abide you

entering such a place of danger. If it is important to you that someone takes a closer look, I will gladly volunteer."

Nodding weakly, she headed toward the barrier with Laniea. The Warrior hesitantly tested the white light, placing her fingertips gently against it. Her hand easily pushed through and her arm quickly followed. Soon her entire being was behind the white light. Emmeldine watched closely from outside the barrier and saw Laniea inching closer and closer to the light sparks within the boulders. Bright red, blue, and green were distinguishable amid a mesh of color. Emmeldine's mouth opened in warning but before she could get anything out, Laniea leaned forward and reached her arm out toward the lights… and was *gone*.

Chapter 26 - A New Queen (Then)

Emmeldine was immersed in too many things. She had tradition and ritual to learn such as caring for her mother's body and protocol for the burial of a royal. Simultaneously, she was trying to stay abreast of the search for Alara and keep close contact with her aunt Claraceit about her baby sister, still unnamed. She also had her father to console, and — despite all her pleas to postpone it — an upcoming coronation. Her mind was so full, and her feelings so varied and intense that she often felt like she was floating. Not really here, not really anywhere else, just... in between.

She felt a moment of clarity while cleaning her mother's body, truly touched by the mortality of the flesh and her own mother's travels through birth, growth, giving life, and demise. Thinking of the elder years her mother did not get to enjoy made Emmeldine weep. Later, she would remember the sharp scent of the sacred soap in the bathing water, the quiet surrounding the drip of rain outside the window, her own heart pounding. She softly placed a hand on her chest to feel her own life force, then put down the sponge. She left her mother for the last time, knowing the burial team would take over and that she would never see her mother's body again. She felt numb.

Two of her mother's advisors tried to prepare her for the transition, but it was all she could do to bleakly nod at their river of words.

"Your own ladies will take our places after the coronation. Recommendations are being made for new advisors from the different regions of our lands. Your first council meeting will occur as soon as the nominees accept. A new rule requires new leaders — although a few of your mother's choosing will remain to offer wisdom and guidance. Do you understand, your Majesty?"

Emmeldine nodded while continuing to stare at a tapestry on the wall. The reds and purples blurred together through her watery gaze.

"We have spies and guards sent out to see about your sisters. Messages have gone out to all of Dono's lands requesting Alara be returned immediately. Inquiry into the health of … of the infant princess has been made. Is there anything else you would like us do in regard to your sisters?"

The red and purple blurs became a liquid pool before her as she shook her head softly.

"Very well, your Majesty, we shall keep you informed. Rest ye well."

The two tall, regal women quietly exited the chamber, allowing the reluctant young monarch to cry freely in peace.

Shaima advised her to take a few more days to grieve fully and then, as she was to be Queen, she would have no choice but to plunge forward and rule. That was the only way it could be. Later on, she would learn that Alara was thought to be with her father in the North, and Emmeldine agreed to leave her be. She also learned that the baby was blessed in ritual by the Goddess under her aunt's care, then had passed away in the night. Emmeldine felt a small pang at that. She knew she should care more, but she couldn't come to terms with the fact that her sister's birth led to her mother's death — and in some ways, to Alara's departure. Her mother and Alara held places of love in her heart. The baby girl was... a stranger, unknown. One day, several fortnights after her mother's passing, Shaima came to her while she aimlessly wandered the gardens.

"Emmeldine, soon to be Queen of Trimeria: we must speak."

Emmeldine sighed and nodded her head, eyes downcast, shoulders slumped.

"I know."

"This is a very trying time for many of us. Your mother was a beloved Queen. She had several males who gave her their hearts, various offspring, and a Queendom that appreciated her for the peace she held and the security she offered. It is time for you to step up — to take her place and lead us all forward. Your people need you, your sister needs you, and the court *especially* needs you. We cannot let discontent rise, we mustn't let any cause for alarm be rung. We need you. Now."

With one last sigh, Emmeldine looked up: big blue eyes fiery with salt, turning an almost luminescent green. She nodded again, this time more confidently.

"I will not let Mother down. I will rule, and I will do so well. I will maintain peace in the land and regain harmony in my family. I will be Queen."

Shaima gave a bow of the head and extended her palms up, hoping the hair that fell into her face hid the small smile she felt plastered there.

"I know you will, Emmeldine. I know you will."

The coronation was a lovely moment, filled with smiles and tears. Emmeldine decided it should be held in the back gardens, where she and her mother had often strolled together. There was only room for an intimate group, but the palace was open afterward to all — there was feasting and celebrating for days. Musicians, entertainers and artisans of all kinds came from all over the realm to pay respect to the new Queen. Emmeldine was comforted by her father's presence, but worried that he would not stay once the celebrations ended. She decided to ask.

"Father?"

"Yes, My Queen?" He smiled proudly at her.

"Oh, Father! I will always be your child. I don't think I will ever feel above you in any way."

"Yet you are my dear, as your mother would remind us all clearly if she were here. You are the ordained ruler, chosen by the Goddess herself. I am but your loyal subject." He bowed lightly, a wicked grin rippling over his lightly wrinkled face.

"Oh, Father! I hope...well, I hope that's true. That I am meant to rule. That I can do this, without Mother. That never was the plan, was it? Not like this…"

"No, not like this. I know for a fact that your mother wanted to see this day, that she planned to pass on the reign when she saw you were ready. She was so proud of you, you know? She was very confident that you would do well when the time came. Of course, no one expected it to be so soon." He wiped at his nose, then eyes with a cloth from his breast pocket.

"What would she have me do about Alara? I have sent for her but she refuses to come. Shall I send for Dono, should I force the matter? Before you answer Father, I must tell you that things did not end well between Alara and I before she left, right before Mother… Well, she was very distressed and hostile with me, and likely had good reason to be. I'm not sure I'm even ready to see her… I don't know what to do."

"I suggest you wait. You sent a royal invitation; she was asked to attend her mother's end of life ceremony and your coronation. It seems obvious to me that she needs more time. Hopefully she will come to her senses soon and return. I'm a bit concerned her father is holding her back, but ultimately she will be the head of their section of the family and she will have to learn to speak for herself. Goddess willing, she will be back behind these castle walls soon enough so we can keep watch over her."

Emmeldine shook her head in confusion at the last but realized that overall, her father was speaking sensibly. She decided she would give Alara what space she needed, then have open arms extended when she wanted to come back to court life. Yes — her arms would be ready. She quickly said a prayer to the Goddess for Alara's safe return, then for the soul of her baby sister, whom in her mind she had named Cleoandra.

Chapter 27 - A Entryway to Nowhere (Now)

Emmeldine couldn't help but cry out when Laniea disappeared. Her shriek was loud and shrill and the others nearby all leapt up, battle ready. Once they saw no immediate threat, they raced to the young Queen's side as she pointed to the rocks: the glow gone, having faded quickly after Laniea passed through.

"Laniea, she was there! She disappeared!" Her face was pale as a bright moon and her hands trembled.

"Shaima said...entryway...gone." She shook and collapsed down to her knees, silent tears streaming down her cheeks.

The others rushed forward and began exploring the rocks, but the lights had faded and gone — no smells or other evidence were present. Just a dark rocky patch as the night turned to dawn. Several birds start to chirp nearby. Their cheerful notes sound like cruel mockery. The others searched the area, moving stones to look for holes or caves, all to no avail. Emmeldine managed to climb up the nearest boulder and Daria came up to rub her shoulder and whisper comforting words. Emmeldine continued to hang her head and be silent. After some time, Daria looked up into her friend's worried eyes and gave a slight nod.

"I know your heart is aching, dear Emmeldine. We won't give up. In the meantime, I wonder if we should hurry back to the palace? Either Shaima will already be there, or you can send for her. Hopefully she will know what to do."

"Of course you are right, yet it is hard to imagine the strength to go on. My core is drained." Emmeldine continued to stare at the ground forlornly for several long moments. " Although… the thought of reigniting the search for Cleoandra does give me a jolt. Yes, we must return quickly. There is much to be done."

The shiny-eyed Queen stood wobbly and accepted her friend's arm for support. They headed over to the ride leader to set the plan into motion. The team was off before the sun broke the horizon.

Several days later they pounded into the palace entry gates, horses covered in dust and panting heavily. Emmeldine hopped down quickly and squealed out loud when Shaima came out the front door straight toward her. The two women hugged tightly and Emmeldine began to weep.

"We lost Laniea. She went into the lights... then she was gone."

"Oh no! Oh my dear, I am so sorry for you. I know you feel responsible."

Emmeldine looked up with swollen red eyes and remained silent.

"Please know, dear Emmeldine, there was no way you could have known and nothing you could have done. If it hadn't been her, it might have been you. The Warriors live and serve to protect the Crown. Laniea, if she really is gone for good, died an honorable death. I have some hope she may still return, hopefully unharmed."

Emmeldine let out another small sob and wiped her eyes. She knew she should not appear too distraught around others, lest they think her incapable.

"Let's go to my chambers and talk. We have much to plan for."

Then Emmeldine, Queen of Trimeria, stood tall and walked proudly into the palace, a strong example to all.

Chapter 28 - The Past (Then)

Several years went by and Alara's location became unknown. She had been granted lands after their mother's death, and it was thought she was hiding out in one of the many estates she held in her keep. There had been reports of her setting up households, a new family crest she created, loyal servants and messengers eager for a touch of royalty in their lives. At first, Dono had kept up correspondence with the court, assuring them all that Alara was in good health and needed more time to heal from the trauma of her mother's death. Later, however, there were no responses... and the sightings of him stopped completely.

Emmeldine, believing her baby sister, whom she thought of as Cleo, dead, tried to focus on her relationship with her father and invited her brothers to come live at the palace. They stayed for some time, but one by one they requested to return to their estate in the country, and Emmeldine was often alone while her father stayed with them. She decided to thrust herself into her new Queendom, to learn the ins and outs of the land and keeping fair rule. To become the most peaceful, wise Queen in the history of Trimeria. All appeared well until the day she decided to take one of her special outings into the surrounding countryside, to luxuriate in a swim before heading back to attend court duties. A messenger arrived with news of her sister, Alara. News she had waited for so long, but was shocked to hear.

Chapter 29 - Back At The Castle (Now)

Emmeldine ended up lying down for a large portion of the day, rising mid-afternoon to meet with her most trusted advisor. Shaima found the Queen on her balcony, contemplating the clear sky.

"Isn't it funny, Shaima, that all we see here is so real to us — it is all we know. Yet there is somewhere else, connected to here, that is just as real? It boggles the mind, truly. How can this be?"

"Perhaps it isn't exactly somewhere else? Perhaps both places are the same, existing at once but apart… I know it is hard to put words around. Like the Fairies' language, there is no translation we can comprehend. I say "entryway to another realm," but really I do not know. I do know that there are many creatures we consider magical, that they are as real as we are. I do not know from where they come or how their bodies work. I am passing on all my knowledge to you. It will be up to you to move forward when my time is done. You are my legacy."

The older woman looked at the young Queen with dewy eyes crinkled and reached out her arms. Emmeldine teared up and thrust herself into her mentor's arms.

"Oh Shaima! No, you mustn't ever leave me. I will be all alone. I need you — you are my family."

Shaima gently pulled away and looked gravely at her friend.

"I am getting on in age and these travels are wearing on me. Please prepare yourself, my dear — I cannot stay with you forever. When the Goddess calls, I am ready to answer."

Emmeldine felt a cold wave flow through her body from head to toe and her shoulders stiffened. Her mind briefly fluttered to thoughts of Tharin, whom she had not seen since her arrival back at the palace, and then returned to this conversation she did not want to be having.

"Come my friend, let's sit in my parlor and talk. You must fill me in and we must plan how to block the entries."

As the ladies sat down, Emmeldine tried not to notice how tired her old friend looked, choosing to ignore the dark circles under her sagging eyes and the fact that her once grey-streaked hair was all but pure white now. White as the snow she had heard rumor of, but had yet to see.

"All right then, tell me about the entry point you found. What happened there?"

"It was terrible. A wretched creature, stronger than the others. We nearly lost to it. I'm not sure what it would have done had we not persevered. This creature was feline in nature, or at least appeared that way to us. It is hard to compare magical creatures to those of our realm. Nevertheless, we referred to it as The Feline afterwards. I glanced quickly at my scrolls and think it might have been a Markel. " Emmeldine's eyes widened and she nodded for her to continue.

"This time in the process of containing it, we accidentally killed the beast. Well, not exactly an accident, I suppose. We were using defensive magic and when it started to overpower us, we switched to offensive. We had no choice. Unfortunately, the creature lit ablaze and we were not able to keep it for study. Perhaps we should send someone back to search for any stray hair or remnants of the canine creature? We must find out all we can about these things." The last was said with a disgusted shake of her head, and a small spray of spittle escapes Shaima's mouth.

"Was the point blocked?" Emmeldine stared intently at her mentor and friend.

"I believe so. I used the methods I recommended to you and the lights disappeared. All was calm. I wonder if we can reopen it to try and pull Laniea out? It would be very risky. Possibly very foolish."

Emmeldine shook her head, the thought of losing anyone else unbearable. She wondered if there was another way.

"Shaima… do you remember an old Crone that used to live in the forest east of here? She may be in the spirit world by now, but she seemed to know a lot about magic."

Shaima's tired eyes rose up and a small scowl licked across her face.

"I knew it! Tartanya got to you, didn't she? I had warned her to stay away. You must remember, your mother was very against the use of magic, especially for royals. I had no choice but to forbid her. I suspected she was around a few times but never had true evidence. For some reason she was very eager to speak with you. What did she say?"

"Oh, not much really… She did help me realize that magic was real. At the time I thought she was making things up to get attention. And… well, I think she was alluding to the part you haven't wanted to share with me. The part you said would change me. Perhaps now is the time?"

Shaima eyed her young Queen warily and thought for a moment.

Emmeldine cleared her throat, "Also, well… there is a chance she knew Alara. If Alara knows things I do not, certainly that puts me at a grave disadvantage?"

Shaima's shook her head as her lips brace tightly together. She let out a muffled groan.

"I'll tell you what I am thinking — there is indeed much I should tell you. And given I feel my time in our realm is ending, I should share it soon." Shaima raised a hand when she saw Emmeldine open her mouth to speak. Emmeldine's lips snapped closed and she nodded. "Let me go gather my things, and more importantly my thoughts, and I will meet with you after the evening meal. Your council wanted a large banquet to celebrate your safe return from what they think were your travels to meet potential mates. I managed to convince them that you are weary and would like a more intimate affair. So of course that means at least 50 people." She chuckled and her wrinkly eyes crinkle with delight. "Besides, I saw Tharin lurking around your halls earlier and I dare say he is outside your door right this very moment, hoping for a word."

"Truly? How do you know?" The Queen strode briskly to her chamber door and thrust it open, startling a peacefully waiting Tharin who was leaning against a wall. Shaima quickly excused herself, giving a bemused look to Emmeldine as she passed and a twinkly-eyed smile to the young male she skirted by.

"Greetings, Tharin. I am surprised to find you here. Might I assume you are waiting for me?"

Emmeldine felt an odd combination of apprehension and arousal as she looked into his warm brown eyes. Her cheeks heated up despite her strong effort to keep her smile neutral and her expression pleasant, yet bland. A mini battle raged inside her core.

"No, m'Lady" He gave a slight bow and looked up with twinkling eyes and a bemused grin. " I was waiting for you, but now that you grace me with your presence I wait no longer. Thank you for that."

At the last his face turned serious and his voice deepened. He looks at her questioningly.

Emmeldine smiled, and a flutter of warmth smoothed her confused body.

"Dear Tharin, I have missed you. Won't you come visit with me for awhile. I could use some comforting companionship if you don't mind."

"I would like nothing more My Queen, nothing at all."

With that, the pair entered the Queen's chambers and shut the doors. Emmeldine gestured for Tharin to sit in one of her plush cushioned chairs and she sat beside him, quietly studying his face.

"Can I assume that you know I was not really traveling the land meeting potential mates? That there was a secret purpose to my travels that had nothing to do with my future family?"

"Aye...Yes, well I had hoped and partially assumed that was the case. But hearing it from you brings quite some comfort... more than it should, I fear." He blushed and looks down.

"Tharin...I know our...our friendship is a bit unusual. I want to be honest with you. I do have feelings for you. Feelings of romance and physical attraction and true friendship too. I...I... think maybe we can be more to each other then I have previously allowed. To do this I need some reassurance — I need to really know who you are. No secrets, no deception. Do you think you can do this?"

Tharin started to stand, then sat back down. His face now fully flushed and his eyes glistening, he looked at Emmeldine intently.

"I want that more than I can say. Emmeldine... may I simply call you Emmeldine when we are alone?"

She nodded.

"I would like nothing more than that, dear Emmeldine. You truly are becoming dear to me. I missed you greatly while you were away. I am very, very glad to hear you were not with another male. You are amazing to me. I have seen you grow up since you were a young lass. I watched. I watch. I do this because it is in my nature and I do this because I am lonely. I was but a lad myself when I came to the palace. You know my mother died in childbirth and my father could not provide for us all. What you don't know is that I was so well trusted that the heads of various parts of the castle vied for my service. *That's* why I learned so much about palace life. I worked in the kitchen, attending the ladies and assisting in the stables."

Emmeldine winced and he suddenly stopped speaking, his head tilted to the side as he examined her face silently. Finally, she extended a hand to indicate he should go on.

"My family never came back for me. I have no one to call my own. Over the years I got to know your family very well. I admired your parents, both very strong and clever in their own ways. I imagined they were my parents at times, and little Alara. I imagined she was my sister. But you

Emmeldine, you I never saw that way. I have always felt a unique pressure in my heart when it comes to you. I feel a connection like no other I have known."

She leaned forward and took his hands between hers... pale, delicate hands trembling around the large sturdy pair. She looked at him with wide eyes, lips pursed together tightly.

"Emmeldine, I know, I know there are so many reasons why we shouldn't be together. Custom and station and lineage and the fact that you obviously have something very serious you are dealing with out in the land and probably need to devote yourself to. All that said... I am here. I love you, I want to be with you. Forever."

Emmeldine squeezed his hands and silent tears started streaming down her face. Her mind had been racing while Tharin spoke, and now she was so confused as to how she could respond... how she *wanted* to respond. Perhaps it was her fatigue and weariness, or the promise of Shaima's impending revelations, or the warmth of Tharin's eyes and hands that caused Emmeldine, Queen of Trimeria and defender against evil magic, to let go of all reservation and follow her heart.

"I love you, too! I want to be with you, too!" She thrust herself forward and landed in his arms. They held each other tightly for several moments. Then she lifted up her head and he lowered his, and they shared a gentle, yet passionate kiss. She quickly pulled back.

"I just...I don't know how to do this. I, too have practically no family. Certainly no mother or sister I can talk to about such things, and my aunts are all far away. I want to figure out if there is hope for us, if there is a way for us to have a future, before things go too far. Do you understand? Can we just continue our friendly companionship for a while longer while I figure this out?"

"Emmeldine, I will do anything you ask. You know how I feel. If you let me touch you, I will. If you let me kiss you, I will. And if you ask me to stay back I can do that as well... but I do want you, in all ways. Let that be known."

He stood up and gazed at her intensely, then gave a big sigh and started to turn away. She jumped up and grabbed his arm, gently turning him toward her. She smiled slyly at him, eyes sparkling blue.

"There is no need to go just yet. Let's talk more about these kisses you want to give me."

Chapter 30 - Awakenings

Later that evening, after the banquet in her honor, Emmeldine headed toward Shaima's rooms, eager to hear all her dear friend could tell her. While striding in that direction, Emmeldine had to constantly fight the urge to turn around and run to Tharin — her body eager for his touches, her lips stinging to be kissed. She felt heat flash through her in an exquisite way, and she had to take a deep breath and try to clear her mind. Emmeldine thought about how much was really on her shoulders right now and reminded herself that she still needed to see if a relationship with Tharin could ever have any potential for future partnership. She didn't want to bind her body with a male she couldn't stay with. She most certainly did not want to be like her mother and use males for pleasure. Realizing that she had reached Shaima's door, she shook her head slightly and breathed deeply again. This was the moment she had long been anticipating, when she would hopefully learn about the mysterious connection between the peoples of her land and the magical creatures from far away. With a last slow breath she leaned forward, gripped the handle, and pulled.

Shaima was halfway across the large room, sitting in a comfortable looking plush blue chair. Her eyes were closed and her chest rose up and down softly. There was a half full cup of tea next to her on a side table with a few fruit slices next to it. Emmeldine guessed she had fallen asleep at afternoon tea time and had been out ever since. She quietly sat down next to her on a hard stool and took her wrinkled hand in her smooth, pale one. Silently she sat and held her friend's hand, gently rubbing her thumb over the loose skin. Emmeldine's mind wandered dangerously. *Could she make a life with Tharin? Was it really her fault Alara was attacking them? What more would come? What could she do?* Her mind started to spin and she felt the room move with it. Taking some deep breaths, Emmeldine decided to move to the other plush chair opposite her friend and close her own eyes for awhile. She was exhausted.

The next morning, Emmeldine and Shaima were both awakened by a pounding at the door.

"Shaima! Open up! Have you seen the Queen?"

More pounding. Emmeldine leapt up while Shaima's eyes snapped open and followed her movements to the door. Emmeldine undid the locks she had put in place the night before to ensure the privacy she thought they had needed for their paramount conversation. Emmeldine's heart gave a lurch even as Daria burst in, realizing that she still does not know whatever it was she had been on the brink of discovering last night.

Daria stopped mid stride as she spotted Emmeldine, noticing her rumpled gown and her hair half-fallen out of yesterday's braids. Her glance flashed to Shaima as she gulped for breath, then continued.

"Emmeldine! You must come at once. Your father himself is here. He has news of Alara! He appeared very worn and incredibly concerned. He wants to speak to you directly and would not tell anyone what this unexpected visit is about."

Emmeldine stood completely still, mouth slightly agape, staring at her childhood friend. Daria quickly brushed her dark curls from her face and leaned forward to grab Emmeldine's hand, gently tugging and leading her out the door. Shaima slowly rose to follow.

Emmeldine's mind reeled as they hurried through the long palace hallways. She attempted to voice some of her thoughts to Daria, which came out in seemingly random gasps.

"Father? Why? Alara… What?" She looked at her friend beseechingly.

"I don't know, hopefully helpful news? Perhaps she visited him? I really do not know. Let's go ask him together."

"Yes. Shaima… Tharin… I want them with me."

"Tharin? Shaima is on her way, she will be shortly

behind us. Why do you need...Oh! Things have changed with you, haven't they? Are you enjoying more than just friendship now?"

Emmeldine glanced at her while she hurried forward, a pained expression on her face.

"It's ok, Emmeldine. You deserve companionship, you deserve love. Whatever happens, I will be by your side. In all ways."

Emmeldine slowed enough to offer a weak smile. "Thank you dear Daria. Thank you."

The two women passed through the final doorway to the parlor Reynaldo was resting in. Emmeldine practically sprinted the final few yards and threw herself at her father, who was rising from a wood bench.

"Father! Oh Father, I am ever so happy to see you, happier then you can know." Her body shook as she squeezed his strong frame.

"Oh my dear, I dare say I do know, and I feel the same." He squeezed her back, then took her hands in his larger ones and looked deeply into her eyes.

"Your sister, she sent a messenger to my estate. A most unpleasant one. He was not like any race I have met before — complexion very pallid, almost green. His?...It's eyes yellow and narrow, voice unlike anything I've ever heard as if being translated through a whistle, and quite an unpleasant smell. He demanded we pledge allegiance to your sister, to pledge to uphold her rule were she to take the crown. Of course we laughed and denied any intention of doing such. Suddenly the male looked more creature-like then before and attacked us! All fought bravely including your brothers, but this... person?...Thing, took your baby brother Damin just a few moon cycles from being a grown male himself. Damin is gone!"

"Oh Father! Oh no! She goes too far! I don't understand. I know she hates me, but surely she has nothing against you and my brothers?" Tears streamed down the young Queen's face.

Daria left quietly as Emmeldine and Reynaldo embraced again and shared tears of sorrow. She headed quickly back toward Shaima's rooms and found her halfway to the parlor. Quickly she filled the old woman in on what has occurred and Shaima ducked her head sadly, shaking it side to side.

"I cannot let any more time pass. I must write out some very important things for Emmeldine. She has so very much to deal with, and this information is vital. I fear… Well, I fear my time is nearly gone. Daria, will you come to my chambers later and retrieve my writings for her? I should be done by tea time."

"Of course I will. Here, let me help you back to your rooms."

Later that morning, after Emmeldine and her father had spoken privately for quite some time, Tharin arrived in the parlor, followed by Daria who had brought him as requested.

"Please sit down, both of you." Emmeldine extended a long, elegant arm toward a couch across from them. The Queen had regained her composure.

Tharin and Daria sat down on the couch, awkwardly trying not to brush limbs with each other. Tharin cleared his throat and smiled at Emmeldine, who was sitting close to her father with her hand in his. Reynaldo looked surprised to see Tharin and gave Daria a quick smile.

"Good to see you again, Daria. You have grown into a strong woman, I see. I want to thank you for staying by my daughter's side during these difficult times. The Goddess has surely blessed her with a friend like you."

"My pleasure, dear sir. Emmeldine, the Queen, is a pleasure to serve. I care for her deeply."

"As we all do, my dear." Reynaldo smiled warmly at Daria, fixed his eyes questioningly on Tharin, then quickly glanced back to his daughter.

Emmeldine smiled tightly and sighed. She knew she needed to be upfront with her loved ones about her intentions so that they could all work together to stop Alara.

"I have asked you here together because I face very dangerous times. Indeed, our entire kingdom does. Two of our beloved have been captured by a mostly unknown enemy, apparently at the command of my sister Alara. You three are the closest to my heart." Emmeldine used all her will to continue after seeing her father gasp and sit up stiffly. "Father, you are all that remains of the family I have known. Daria, you have been my dearest friend and confidant over the years, and Tharin, you have become my companion and my comfort. I need you all. After talking to my father at length about what has occurred in his home region, I have come to the conclusion that there must be a entryway near there. I intend to head toward that area, recruiting along the way anyone who may have a propensity for magic or for bronze, and search for the entry point. Once we find it, I intend to lure Alara there. I am truly not sure which side of the opening she is on. Can our kind even survive in their realm? There is much we do not yet understand. That said, I will attempt to enter that realm if I must. No...Stop!" She gestured for everyone to sit down and they all jumped up and started to argue with her.

"That's ridiculous!"

"Absolutely not!"

"I will not be ordered around, in this I will be Queen! I am the only one strong enough in magic and knowledgeable enough about Alara to save my brother and our Warrior friend. This cannot continue, these attacks. I have to put an end to it, if at all possible."

Emmeldine's tense voice, raised louder than anyone present had heard before, was enough to stop them from interrupting. As soon as her speech paused, they all started to talk at once.

"Surely there is another way..."

"You cannot be serious!"

"Immensely dangerous."

She raised a palm up and looked at them all intently. "This is the basic plan, my dears. It is time Alara and I end this...this feud between us. If given a chance, I would like to apologize to her — to see if there is any hope of us being sisters again. If nothing else, the time for confrontation has come, and we must move forward. Please keep in mind, entering the other realm is a very unlikely outcome. I will first try everything in my power to communicate with her and to stop any further attacks. The last thing I want is to leave all of you. I wish very dearly to be here with you all and have a peaceful future."

Her sparkling eyes, almost green with the salty tears welling up in them, looked directly at Tharin.

That evening, Emmeldine and her group of magic users and special Warriors prepared for an early morning departure. Emmeldine had checked on Shaima earlier and the older woman was asleep. She decided not to ask Shaima to join them; it was too risky. Emmeldine was very reluctant to go on this journey without her mentor, but she knew it could be the downfall of her aging friend. She was not willing to risk that. She was just putting her final special items into a case when she heard a soft knock on her chamber door. After verbally granting entry, the heavy door swung open and Tharin stood looking at her silently with serious eyes.

"I am so very glad you came! I'm sorry I could not meet alone with you after I was with Father. I feel great haste to be off and stop Alara before anyone else can be harmed. If it were up to me, we would leave this eve... but my group needs more time to prepare." She stepped forward and raised her arms to him, and he immediately stepped into her embrace.

"I understand. I too have been preparing. I want to come with you. Please, don't say no!" He pulled back and took her hands in his, rubbing his thumb against her skin in a way that made it tingle.

"Tharin! This will be very dangerous, and… well, you are a male. I can't worry about you losing control of your emotions. Anger would be very dangerous in this situation."

"I know this, and I know that you are a proponent of male equality, albeit still somewhat secretly. Emmeldine, I have had some training. I am not an aggressive male. I have never raised my voice in malice nor have I struck a living being. I swear to you, I can do this. Please, it would be torture to be here without you, and if these are to be our last days together, for whatever reason, well… then I want to spend them … together." He looked up at her with smoldering eyes, and pulled her into his firm embrace.

"I...I want to spend them with you, too. If you swear you are ready, that you can truly handle what is to come, then yes, I will take you. After all I have told you these last few days... you understand that we are talking about facing magical creatures? That I myself can use defensive magic?"

He looked down at her with adoring eyes and smiled faintly. "I always knew you were special. I remember it always seemed like you were more capable than others girls your age. You could hear better, smell more, see farther. It comes as little surprise to me that you can do magic. And I am relieved to hear that your magic thus far has only been for defending yourself and others. I will pray to the Goddess that is all it shall ever be."

"Aye," She barely whispers, looking down. "I shall pray for that as well." The next morning there were teary goodbyes as Emmeldine and her father prepared to part once again.

"Part of me wants to join you, but I feel desperate to get back to your brothers, lest anything else go awry. I do fear for you too, my dear. It is wrong to risk my Queen daughter's life, even to save my own son. Promise me you will be cautious, that you will not give your life for his?"

"Oh, Father! My every intention is for us all to come home safe and whole. I know it may seem reckless, but you must trust me when I say this thing between Alara and I can only be solved with my presence."

"I trust you, my dear. It is *her* I have no faith in."

"I have a wonderful team going with me. Unfortunately, Shaima is ailing. I did not want to wake her, but I was assured that Daria was able to retrieve some vital information from her in writing before she departed with the advance team last night. They are going to scout the countryside around your estate to look for signs of Alara or her minions."

"What is this Shaima is meant to have written for you?" Reynaldo's mouth tightened.

"I am actually quite eager to read Shaima's words and hope they will help me figure out how to get my sweet brother back." Her heart nearly froze at the thought of him suffering by evil hands. "Shaima said she had certain truths to tell me, about magic users and race. I must be off, Father, but rest assured I shall fill you in when I can. I will do everything in my power to return my brother to you safely. I promise."

"Of course you will my love, my heart. Of course you will."

Emmeldine mounted her mare, her slick riding clothes made of animal hide sliding gently over the sleek black hairs of her horse's back. She adjusted a light hood over her hair and hoped she could pass inconspicuously through her lands. She glanced over at Tharin, who was adjusting his own gear on a mare next to her. She admired his muscled body as he twisted to tie a strap. He turned back and caught her gaze. A slow, sensual smile crept across his face, and his eyes held hers for a moment. The sounds of the rest of the group departing broke their connection and with a small sigh, Emmeldine locked her eyes on the Warrior in front of her and directed her horse to follow.

They rode hard through the fields and forests, following the least-known paths to avoid encountering people and causing concern. Reynaldo's estate was about a day's journey from the palace, and they planned to meet up with the advance team just west of there to spend the night and formulate their plan. As they rode, Emmeldine thought about what might be in the letter from Shaima. She knew it somehow had to do with magic and with Emmeldine herself. She tried not to worry that the information would be something unpleasant or challenging. She dared hope that it could be something very helpful to the current cause, perhaps something wonderful.

It was impossible to talk while riding fast, so she and Tharin took turns looking toward each other and smiling. At first Emmeldine was nervous to show open affection to him around her team, but then she realized that if she could trust the team to fight magical creatures, she could surely trust them with this… friendship? Romance? She still wasn't quite sure where it could go.

They rode long and hard, stopping only twice for brief breaks. During these few moments where feet were touching ground, Emmeldine struggled not to thrust herself into Tharin's arms. She wanted comfort desperately. She couldn't stop thinking about her brother and Laniea being trapped with the enemy, possibly gone forever. Her mind also flashed to Shaima, and she worried she might never see her dear friend and and most trusted advisor again. She felt tears stinging like a pricklefly and swatted at them as such. Tharin walked over from where he had been consulting with a Warrior and gently took one of her hands in his. He softly rubbed his thumb against her palm and she immediately felt her body soften. She didn't realize how incredibly stiff and tight she felt until his touch. She offered a weak smile and he looked deeply into her eyes.

"It's going to be ok, Emmeldine. We will find them. Please keep faith. I am here for you, we all are here for you."

Emmeldine looked around, realizing the surrounding

hum of conversation had gone still. All of her traveling group, friends and Warriors alike, were looking at her and smiling. Their eyes showed only love and concern. These were people she could trust. She smiled back, her whole face softening, and she squeezed Tharin's hand tightly. She opened her mouth to speak, surprised by how much effort it took to speak a few words softly.

"Thank you all, I value and absorb your friendship. Let us continue on our journey."

With one last squeeze of Tharin's hand, she gently turned away and mounted her mare, her smile turning to a look of determination. They must reach Estaridge, her father's estate, before nightfall and find a way to save her brother. She could not fail.

Chapter 31 - Siblings

As they rode hard once again, Emmeldine thought back to when she and Alara were still playmates and their brothers had come to the palace for one of their rare visits. Damin must have been barely more than a babe and Ladin had been a feisty youth, exploring every nook and cranny of the gardens and nearby woods. And Treyu, he was a quiet child who rarely played with the other children in the castle and sought out his big sister regularly. Alara was thrilled that she had new playmates and took great pride in showing her brothers all the things she knew about the palace and its people. Alara seemed particularly attached to their baby brother. She would often voice how much older she was than he and would try to nurture and mother him as much as possible. Emmeldine found it very sweet to see her little sister caring for a younger child. Emmeldine remembered enjoying this visit greatly, not having seen her brothers since the birth of Damin. She also knew that one of the reasons for their arrival was so that her father could try to impregnate her mother with another daughter. Her mother seemed obsessed with having at least two legitimate female heirs.

Emmeldine did not understand why her brothers could not be heirs, and did not particularly understand why more children were needed if she was expected to rule one day. She did not often think about becoming Queen; that notion felt like a very hazy dream remembered upon waking, like it wouldn't ever really happen. Her mother Maraleine was Queen and that was how it should be. Emmeldine simply wanted to be with her entire family and learn about the world.

She found the natural happenings fascinating and would stay after her lessons asking her teachers many questions. There were never enough answers.

Alara at this time was quite adventurous. She was known to flee her minders and wander the grounds and was

often found in the kitchen pantries or near the basement
doors. Dono had been sent off on a peacekeeping mission
shortly before Reynaldo arrived with the boys, so Alara had
fewer grown eyes on her then she was used to. She quickly
took advantage of this. One day, all the royal children had
been outside playing in the hedge maze. Ladin was quietly
digging at the ground, examining insects. His red hair,
lighter and thinner than Emmeldine's, blew in the gentle
breeze as his blue eyes watched a tiny, slimy round creature
slither slowly toward him. The eldest brother Treyu was
excitedly calling out to his sisters, running ahead and hiding.
His tall, lean frame was muscled and he had the same
coloring as all his siblings. The baby (as they often referred
to Damin) had been behind a bush with Alara, loudly calling
out in his soft, whispery baby voice, "Here! Here!" Alara
tried to quiet him by putting her hand on his mouth and he
started crying. She tried to explain to him they were hiding
and Damin wailed louder. He started to swat at her with his
chubby little hands and she put her hands up to defend
herself. Damin fell backward, landing on his heavily-clothed
bottom and screamed loudly, then pushed himself up slowly
and ran off. Emmeldine remembered the look on Alara's
face: she appeared both very perplexed and very ashamed.
Alara briskly followed after Damin and found him quickly.
She gently picked him up and planted soft kisses all over his
dusty face, whispering softly into his ear. Emmeldine never
knew what she had said.

The riders were approaching their rendezvous
destination, so they slowed their pace. They were in a large
meadow that went on as far as the eye could see. Flowers of
blue, red, and yellow dotted the small hills slicked with
green growth. There were some small trees and rocky areas,
but the visibility was good and they felt reassured that
nothing could sneak up on them. Emmeldine longed to go

further, to see her remaining brothers and embrace them tightly. She sighed, knowing she must follow the agreed-upon plan and that her brothers had been moved for their safety to a location she was not aware of. As she slowed her horse, she did not see the advance team waiting. She glanced over at Tharin for reassurance, and he gave her a big smile. They stopped and watered their horses, then stretched and snacked on nuts and dried berries from their packs. The group was mostly quiet, keeping their ears open for approaching sounds. Emmeldine let out an audible sound of relief and touched Tharin's arm as they all saw the advance team coming over the horizon.

Daria pulled ahead of the other advance team members and raced her stallion up to the waiting party. Emmeldine and Daria embraced tightly, and the Queen began to tremble.

"I was so worried for you! I don't think I could go on if something else happened to someone I love. Is everyone well?"

Daria's eyes flickered to Tharin with a surprised expression, then quickly back to her friend. "Yes, yes, all are well. We have very little to report, really. The entry was closed upon our arrival and has not reopened. Ladin and Treyu are confirmed to be safe at the Prelar estate a few hours' ride from here. No sign of Damin or of his captor. I am so sorry."

Daria ducked her head and put her hand to her heart, giving a slight bow.

"I see." Emmeldine's eyes filled with tears and she felt Tharin's warm body press up behind her as he softly put a hand on her shoulder.

"Well then, shall we all go forward to my father's estate? Perhaps there is something that can be done with magic?"

Daria looked up at her friend with hardened eyes. "I dare say there is. I do hope you will forgive me, but I took it upon myself to read Shaima's words, lest there be something there written that would aid us in our mission."

Emmeldine's eyes widened and her breath quickened — she gave a slight nod.

"It seems... well, there is a lot of information. Very important information that you should read yourself and process. I... I'm not sure it's appropriate to discuss here, in front of all."

Once again Daria's eyes flickered to Tharin, then back to the concerned face of her friend the Queen.

"Well then... let us go to the estate, shall we? I imagine my father's study is a good place to take in words."

"Oh yes, it is a lovely home indeed. You will be quite comfortable there. I shall let the others know."

Daria turned to leave and Emmeldine quickly reached out her hand to grasp Tharin's cool fingers. He wrapped them around hers and gave a tight squeeze.

Chapter 32 - The Truth

As they approached Estaridge, Emmeldine took in the sprawling buildings, quite elaborate by normal standards but perfectly suiting for the Queen's mate. Tall rock walls led up to towering turrets and dark vines of eager leaves grasped its sides like a hungry babe. There were etchings on the lower walls that were roughly the height of a tall woman. The etchings were very circular — spiraling shapes that rose and bobbed like currents. Emmeldine though she could make out figures in the spirals... *patterns, maybe?* It was hard to tell with all the vines.

As they dismounted, several brave servants who had volunteered to stay behind when the remaining princes left came out to greet them. Daria headed off with them to make arrangements for the Queen's comfort and Emmeldine shook her head lightly. She didn't like a fuss to be made for her. She smiled lightly at Tharin and started into her father's home, alone.

Emmeldine vaguely remembered the layout from a visit long ago — one of the few her mother allowed her. She took a sharp left immediately after entering the large wood doors and followed a short hall to her father's study. The doors creaked as she gently pushed them open, dust flying up to greet her. The speckles were flickering almost like stars in the sunlight that streamed through the nearby window. The study was large and full of bookshelves. There were some comfortable-looking chairs embroidered in her father's colors of green and blue. A small marble slab with a more sturdy chair was against the far wall with several wall sconces nearby: Reynaldo's writing area.

Emmeldine headed toward it and noticed everything was covered in thick dust. She wondered why the study was not used anymore. Emmeldine had a sudden flash of a memory strike her by surprise — a time when she was fully mature but not yet a fully grown woman. This was probably the last visit she'd had at Estaridge before her mother's death and becoming Queen. She remembered her mother had not yet announced her pregnancy, but there was suspicion. Emmeldine had been allowed a rare visit with her brothers with the understanding that her father would return to the Palace with her afterward. Emmeldine had gotten settled and had tea, then had gone to seek her father in his study. She found him at his desk hunched over some very ancient-looking texts.

"What are you up to, Father? You look so very serious."

"Ah, Emmeldine! You took me by surprise. Oh, I was just looking at some old family heirlooms passed down from my mother's side. She was a great woman, your Grandmother. I wish you could have known her."

"I do as well, Father. May I sit and look?" Emmeldine gestured to a small marble bench near Reynaldo's wooden chair and he nodded his head slowly.

Reynaldo laughed softly as Emmeldine sat on the bench, crossing her legs in her velvety leggings and looking up at him expectantly.

"Your grandmother, Merelda, she was strong. Her spirit was swift and fierce to those who opposed her, but loving and kind to all who allowed it. Things just seemed to always go in her favor. Land disputes were always won by her, games of chance went her way, and her houses and lands flourished."

"It sounds as if the Goddess favored her. She was blessed."

"Aye, that may very well be. Some said otherwise. They speculated that she used magic — they accused her of manipulation and ill gain. At the same time, my family openly spoke against magic, rejecting its existence and claiming it unnatural to aspire to. My mother had great plans for me to marry royalty, you see, and she knew the royal family did not abide by talk of magic."

"Have you discovered something about this in the

texts, then? Is that why you speak of this now?"

" I... well, I'm not sure you should know about all this yet. There were secrets in our family, as I guess all the great families of Trimeria could probably claim. Yet... these secrets are such that they may cause great unhappiness. I don't want to make life harder for any of my children, especially not for you, as you have the burden of ruling our great lands to contend with one day. Nothing is more important than keeping the peace. Nothing."

"Why is that, Father? The realm has been peaceful for a very long time, has it not? What is there to fear?"

"This is true. Yet it wasn't really so long ago that there was great war. Well now, you know how males used to rule the lands. The leaders were hungry for power and led by greed and anger. They had large tribes that feuded and... things got out of control. The wise women of the time banded together to overthrow the men and bring peace to the realm. There is speculation and rumor to this day about how all that really took place. My family goes back to some of the original women who started this movement for change. I believe this is a large part of why I was picked to partner with your mother."

Reynaldo lifted a hand up to his slightly wrinkled brow, his eyes sagging and tired. He looked like he had been studying the texts for days.

"I don't understand, Father. Are you saying these texts hold that truth, that they explain what happened back then?"

"Possibly. I know your mother likes to stick to what the tutors teach all noble girls — she doesn't want to learn any uncomfortable truths. I am starting to wonder though, might these truths help us? Perhaps accurate information is always more valuable than assumptions or misinformation? I also wonder if the truth might help your brothers."

"Help them? In what way? Are they unwell?"

"No no, nothing like that, but I do fear for them. They are not treated equally with you at all, not even with your half sister." At the last he sniffed and squinted. "Your brothers are lovely! They are smart, loving, kind and creative. I believe they deserve every opportunity to flourish. I hate to see them kept away from court most of their lives."

"Oh, Father! I hadn't thought of it as such. Please, let me help. I promise you that even if I cannot change Mother's mind on such matters, that I, when *I* am Queen, shall treat my brothers equal to any princess. They shall have all rights and privileges thereof. I will bring them to the palace and they shall indeed flourish!"

"My dear Emmeldine, light of my light, how I do love you. Yes, child. Thank you. You have given some peace to your old Father's heart."

Emmeldine's cheeks flushed hot and pink and she felt her heart swell. She would not let her father down. With her newfound purpose, she hugged her father and bounced out of the study. The young princess completely forgot about her father's ancient texts. Until now.

Emmeldine enjoyed some refreshments in the study and slowly perused the shelves with eager eyes. There was a faded lilac animal hide bound book on a shelf high above her head. Her breath caught as she recognized the dusty old thing and noticed spiraling designs faintly embedded in the cover. *What do those mean?* Reynaldo's words started to clatter through her mind, then suddenly she turned to the doorway, hearing a soft squeak as it slowly opened. Curly dark hair and solemn shiny eyes greeted her.

Daria walked in quietly, holding a small pile of folded parchment paper. She offered a faint smile to Emmeldine and wordlessly lifted her hands toward her, as if offering the parchment in sacrifice. Emmeldine took a deep breath and slowly reached for them, fingers closing around the crinkling paper softly.

"Thank you."

Chapter 33 - Words Have Meaning

After Daria excused herself, Emmeldine found a more comfortable chair and sat down softly as a small poof of dust flew toward her expectant eyes. She coughed and tried to wave the flecks away. *Why didn't her father have this room cleaned?* She slowly tucked her legs up and under, looked around the room slowly, and finally down at the papers she held loosely in her cool, dry fingers. The information she was about to read felt very important, possibly life-altering according to Shaima. She wouldn't dare risk damaging them.

Gently she pulled off the first sheet, which was blank but for the one word written boldly in its center: EMMELDINE. Her breath caught as she took in the page of densely written words. They swam before her like an endless river.

You are my dearest friend during my final days Emmeldine, as I tried to be for your mother during hers. Of course even I did not know she was near her end. Unlike your mother, I have great confidence that you are ready to hear the truth. Wars have been fought, many lives lost over what I am about to tell you. It is not to be taken lightly. I will pray to the Goddess every day I have left to grant you wisdom and strength so that you may use this information to help and not harm, and to hopefully lead our people to a better tomorrow.

The fact is, Emmeldine, magic has been around since the beginning of time, and used to hold a much bigger role in how our world worked. You may have noticed that there are several distinct-looking groups of people in Trimeria. These are not merely physical traits handed down through families. Take you, for example. You are long and lean, fair complexion, red hair and blue eyes. You are directly descended from Elves."

Emmeldine dropped the papers and gasped. Her heart started to race and her palms tingle. She had the oddest sensation of being both shocked and instantly accepting at the same time. Her body hummed with the truth. Her mind began to race, wondering what this information really meant, and she decided to plunge forward with the rest of Shaima's writing before she lost her nerve. Very gently, she gathered the papers and let her wide eyes take in more words.

Your people come from the other realm, as do most of the people you see and interact with on a daily basis. There are most certainly pure "natives" somewhere in this world who have no magical ancestry, but they are in lands far away and I myself have never met them. The people of our lands are not purely descended from one specific magical creature; they had bred with other beings and with the natives, so their magic is faded at best. Only royalty and nobility are nearly pure Elf.

Another example is Dono. His people are descendants of Dwarves. I believe you read about them during our studies of magic. They are a strong, prideful people who are very skillful with their hands and tools, and are prone to anger quickly and act out emotionally. Sound familiar? They also have magic humming in their blood and can access it through their craft.

There are more, but I will stop there for now. There is so much to tell you. The information I am going to share has been passed down from the women in my family for as long as we can remember. I cannot personally verify any of it — but my life experiences, especially those of the last few moon cycles, have proven them true. My intention here is to tell you the most relevant information, with great hope that we will have several more opportunities to talk in person.

Very long ago, in ancient times, there was an exodus from the magical realm to that which we now inhabit. The magical creatures had enjoyed harmony for millennia but were slowly evolving and there started to be some groups who became more cerebral. They started to question the basic order and wanted to expand their own groups, seeking more power. At this time there were a very special group of magical beings called Ethereals. The Ethereals were a tribe of peacekeeping beings who were nearly all-powerful. There is much I would like to tell you about them and their lore, but in the interest of time, I will skip right to what you need to know. There's only one Ethereal left that I know of, the only one who has survived the changes and can cross through each realm. The Goddess.

Emmeldine's shuddered and almost dropped the papers. Only the need to know more was stronger than her shock. She held the papers tightly, then seeing the resulting creases, she lightened her grip while trying to remember to breathe. *The Goddess is a being from the other realm? The last of her kind? How can this be? The Goddess is the supreme being, the one who created all. Or so we thought.* Emmeldine blinked rapidly several times and took a deep breath. She glanced down at the writing but was hesitant to read more. She considered pausing for now and reading the rest another time, but she knew the information could be vital to finding her brother and Laniea. She dared not wait.

The Goddess used to cross over and help our people quite frequently, hence the worship of her that started many generations ago. Around the time of my grandmother's grandmother's grandmother she starting fading from our world, her interventions unfelt. It was the Goddess who helped us realize males were too violent to hold power — she deeply wanted our realm to be more peaceful then hers was becoming. She helped the original queens gain and retain power, bringing an unprecedented peace to our lands. It is because of this that I have given her my loyalty as well. But now... well, my dear Emmeldine, I hate to say that I am questioning this. Does the Goddess truly have our best interests at heart? Why has she abandoned us? Does she even continue to exist? I'm afraid I will be leaving you with many questions, and knowing you, you will seek the truth.

There is one more thing, a prophecy. The Ethereals handed down wisdom to our people, and the last of this I know of was about your mother and her heirs. There was a prophecy that your mother would have a second heir, a girl, and that this girl would bring a new era to the realm. She believed very deeply that this was meant to be. I have often wondered… well, let's hope we can discuss this soon.

Oh, how I so wish we could sit and talk for hours about these matters. Perhaps if your quest goes swiftly and well, I will still be here when you return. I do hope so. I have learned to love you like a daughter, and I am honored to pass down to you the knowledge that has only been allowed to my line. Now you are the keeper. Do with this as you will. Be wise. With great love, Shaima.

Emmeldine's eyes burned and she just barely moved the parchment in time before the first hot, heavy drops fell onto her lap. Her head ached with the tumble of thoughts rolling through it. *Elves…Dwarves… the Goddess? Is the Goddess merely another magical creature, not their creator as they have always believed? Why did the magical creatures want to come to this land and why did so few of them stay? What were her people beyond Elves and Dwarves, were there other groups?* She started to see black dots before her eyes and she feared she might faint. Just then, she heard a knock at the door and shook her head quickly, regaining some vision and ability.

"Wait! Stop! I need to be alone, please leave!"

"Emmeldine? Are you well? Might I please come in?"

At the sound of Tharin's concerned voice, Emmeldine ached for comfort.

"Yes, no one else. Just you."

Later that day, after hours of being silently held by Tharin and a brief nap, Emmeldine decided she had no choice but to move forward with finding her brother. Tharin had been more than generous in his comforts, not asking a thing and merely providing steady arms to hold her and some reassuring words that he was there for her. The young Queen knew this wasn't the time to fall apart. She had to be strong and she had to lead. Hopefully she would have time soon to fully reconcile with Shaima's message.

She found her group in the dining chamber enjoying a large meal. She sat down between Tharin and Daria and sampled some of the beautiful fruit straight from her father's orchards. A sip of ale and a small drip of calm. It felt amazing. She began to pick up on the conversation around her and realized there was a possible entry point not far away. New reports of lights, sounds, and smells were coming in from the local townsfolk.

"How long will it take us to get there? I want to go tonight!"

A chorus of protests broke out.

"Must plan…"

"Too hasty"

"Mustn't rush into…"

"Enough!" She said sternly. "This is not up for group discussion. I for one will be going this eve and I hope some of you will join me. If not, I understand." She stood and looked around the hall with lips pinched together.

Both Tharin and Daria returned her gaze with wide eyes, their frowns betraying their reluctantly nodding heads. Most everyone at the table agreed to join her and they quickly made a plan, two of the Warriors heading off to ready the supplies. They decided to go on foot and leave their exhausted horses in the stables to rest.

Emmeldine silently scanned her memory. *Elves… what were elves good at?* She remembered reading that Elves were connected to nature, a type of mind communication that allowed the Elves to fully submerge with their surroundings and reap the benefit of what the habitat had to offer. They shared a special relationship to animals, communicating naturally and maintaining harmony with even the most fearsome creatures. She felt there was more but she couldn't quite recall. Like the ghost of a dream after being woken from an exhilarating slumber.

As they walked out the front gates, Tharin caught up to her and gently took her hand. "Emmeldine, I... I know you don't wish to be questioned. Please believe I say this only for the care I feel in my heart for you. Please reconsider. What is the rush? Might we rest and plan well, then journey on the morrow? I'm worried for you. You have endured so much...most of which I don't even know. You need rest and care. I wish to help."

"You already have Tharin — your touch, your comfort. I thank thee. It is true I have endured much, and I fear much more is to come. I cannot rest until I know I have done everything in my power to help my brother and Laniea. Furthermore, we must prevent any more attacks. I cannot bear to have anyone's blood on my hands."

"I pray you never do... oh, how I pray." He bowed his head of thick, brown hair and then took her hand and squeezed it. She tried to smile.

Dusk turns to dank night as the group moved quietly through fields and sparse clumps of trees, over a rocky hillside, and down into a small valley surrounded by thick brush and sporadic tall trees. Just ahead, they make out a faint glow and cautiously approach it from several sides, creeping slowly. Emmeldine, Tharin and several Warriors venture from the West and Daria leads the others from the East. A loud screech tore through the night and a large group of bats flew overhead. Hearts pounding, they continued — slowly, slowly closer. Another loud wail, and just as Emmeldine convinced herself it was another forest-dwelling creature, she saw the eyes: glowing, amber, not of this realm.

"Wait!" she hisses, "There it is." She didn't bother to clarify what "it" might be. The others had already stopped cold in their tracks upon seeing the haunting orbs. More shrieks echoed out at them. Emmeldine felt oddly reassured, for the being did indeed seem to be animal in nature. Perhaps her Elf magic could convince it to succumb, or at the worst, to defeat it.

"*Iks nay maloy terra. Boyvay nartunie. Feesom do marfey alla,*" she started chanting softly, then increased in intensity and speed.

"*Iks nay maloy terra. Boyvay nartunie. Feesom do marfey alla,*" A white glowing wall was forming before them, translucent yet cloudy.

The chanting continued and the creature howled again. Suddenly, Daria's voice joined the Queen's and the white intensified and thickened, barely allowing the silhouette of the creature to be seen. A piercing snarl and the sounds of pounding feet rang out as the creature leapt at the wall, then shrieked painfully. Smoke wafted up and a rotten smell of charred flesh assaulted their nostrils. A large thunk was felt as the creature fell to the ground. Emmeldine looked at Daria with surprise, ceasing to chant. Daria immediately followed suit and the two women stood staring at each other for a heartbeat that held its own conversation. The creature convulsed and they quickly turned their attention to it. Emmeldine cautiously stepped closer, feeling Tharin reach out to touch her back. She continued forward and saw the creature's eyes were shut, its form completely slumped. It was no more.

It was hard to make out the coloring in the dark, but it appeared feline in nature, approximately as long as their tallest male and as thick as two horses. This was a fierce beast. Emmeldine had felt her heart drop upon realizing it was dead, but now that she examined it more closely, she realized this outcome was probably the most desirable.

The other team reached them and they lit their lanterns, revealing a thick soft-looking brown coat and two very large fangs protruding from the face. The claws were nearly as big as her hands. She reached out to touch the thick fur, its brown warmth strangely inviting. As her fingers made contact, there was a silent poof of ash and the creature disappeared. They covered their faces, then waved away the last few specks. As the final bits fell, they noticed a single sheet of parchment on the ground where the beast had lain. Emmeldine quickly scooped it up and gasped out loud when she saw its message.

Dear Sister,

Take this as your final warning. Two fortnights from now I will come to take what should have been mine. Ready your troops, prepare what you may. Your rule nears its end. If you want your brother returned safely, then bring me my baby sister. Do not fail.

The message was not signed, but Emmeldine received its meaning all the same. She felt a cold tingling wash through her body and she realized she was holding her breath. She felt nearly frozen but somehow was able to turn back to the group. It was time to return home to the palace. She could only hope that Shaima would be there upon their return. Quickly scouring the area, they confirmed the lights were all gone and no entryway seemed to be present. They quickly headed back to Estaridge, this time tromping loudly without heed through the wilds.

Chapter 34 - To Give Or Receive Death

After a brief rest at Estaridge, the party quickly journeyed home. Emmeldine practically flew off her horse upon entering the palace gates and raced up the spiraling stairs to Shaima's rooms. Barely acknowledging anyone else in the halls, she grasped the thick bronze handles of the doors and thrust them open, her body stumbling forward. She cried out loudly upon seeing her dear friend sitting up in bed, sipping some broth. Tears started streaming down her face as her lips stretched upward and her skin began to glow.

"Shaima! Thank the Godd... Well, thank goodness you are alive! You will never believe what has happened. I have so much to ask. Who else walks among us? Who created life if not the Goddess? What.." Emmeldine paused as her eyes caught up with her mouth. Shaima was looking quite unwell, barely able to slump into her pillow after weakly lowering her spoon. Emmeldine's skin turned to ice and all her functions seemed to slow to the bare minimum. Her heart beat so slowly she was afraid she might die first. She suddenly remembered the other thing that had changed when the women took over power from the men. The males used to leave suffering people to die slow, horrible deaths, thinking it immoral to purposefully end a life. The women instantly acknowledged the cruel irony in this — the men killed all the time for other reasons. Womankind, or at least its rulers, decreed right away that when a person is suffering from advanced old age or an incurable illness, they would be allowed to die with aid. Emmeldine could see with her tired eyes that Shaima was at that point.

"Happy...see you. You read....? Are....well?" Shaima's broken words came out quietly, spittle dripping down her chin. Emmeldine felt furious. *Where were the Healers to help her?* As if reading her mind, Shaima offered a weak, lopsided grin. She very slowly said, "I am... care for....happy...ready...love you."

Emmeldine's face softened and she smiled back. She knew her friend was ready.

"I will get the herbs."

The only other time Emmeldine had experienced a compassionate death was at that of her own grandmother. She was fairly young and Alara was but a babe in the nursery. Her mother's mother had seized being Queen some time before and was referred to as the Queen Mother, a title of respect for both having once been Queen and for having borne the current ruler.

Emmeldine simply knew her as Quema, although she later learned her proper name was Trelina Trimeria, Ninth Queen of the land. As her Quema lay ill in bed, the ravages of old age were apparent. Her skin was thin and drooped, her eyes hazy and watered easily. Emmeldine thought her Quema so interesting, so beautiful. She did not see anything else in her surrounding that displayed this type of decay. She was usually surrounded by lovely, nearly perfect people and objects. She found her Grandmother's decay fascinating.

One cool spring day when the clouds were hazy and the flowers were only just starting to poke through the moist ground, Emmeldine was summoned from her playroom by one of her minders and escorted to her Quema's chambers. She quietly entered and saw her mother standing near the bedside, crushing what looked to be herbs in a small marble bowl. Her mother gestured for her to come to her, and Emmeldine quickly walked to her side. She immediately sensed the importance of the gathering and stood quietly nearby, not asking her normally inquisitive questions. Her mother looked at her briefly and Emmeldine thought she saw tears in her bright blue eyes. This in itself was shocking; her mother was a rock.

"It is time for your grandmother to pass on to the

Goddess. She will feel no pain. She will be surrounded by her loved ones now and then will immediately be held in the Goddess' loving embrace. There is nothing to fear. Say goodbye to her now Emmeldine."

Emmeldine felt an internal panic. *Wait!* she wanted to shout, *how do you know the Goddess will catch her? Can't we wait?* She stood silent for a moment, her feet frozen to the spot as if stuck in the worst of the cook's porridge. After what felt like days, she finally stepped closer to her Quema and gently picked up one of her grey, wrinkly hands.

"I love you Grandmother. Goodbye."

Young Emmeldine was not allowed to stay to watch her Grandmother's final moments. She did, however, turn around right as the door started to close behind her, glimpsing her mother gently rubbing the crushed herbs into her mother's mouth, an expression of tenderness across her often cold features. Emmeldine vowed to herself in that moment that if her mother ever needed assistance in finding peace she would be there for her, rubbing the herbs gently into her mouth as a dutiful daughter should. Of course... she never got that chance.

It crossed Emmeldine's mind to try some healing magic on Shaima, but looking at her dear friend, she knew her time had come. There was no point in delaying the inevitable. Perhaps the Goddess would not be waiting for her, but Emmeldine could plainly see her friend was advanced in age and her frail body done with this realm. Emmeldine tried not to worry about where Shaima's spirit would go after leaving her body. She told herself it must be a better place.

As she sought out the herbs, she noticed a flurry of activity around the palace. Apparently, the word of impending attackers had gotten out and preparations were already underway. She was pleased about this even as her heart was grieving the impending loss. Emmeldine took as many hidden routes as she could to get all she needed. She could not bear to be distracted with possible war during this deeply spiritual moment. She also wanted to avoid Tharin, as she really needed to do this alone. Finally, having gathered up what she needed in a small velvet sack, Emmeldine quickly walked back to the east hall and up the stairs to Shaima's rooms.

Entering quietly, she found the dear woman asleep. Shaima's chest gently rose, her breath rattling softly. Emmeldine wanted to pray, as had been such a large part of her life so far, yet she did not know whom to focus her devotion. She decided she would send good, loving energy out into the universe. *Surely there is more to this all than the crude parts we see before us.*

After her concentrated thoughts of love and harmony, she gently held Shaima's hand, much as she had with her Grandmother all those years ago. She gently leaned over, careful not to disturb the bedding, and placed a single soft kiss on her cheek. Shaima's face remained peaceful, her lips slightly curving upward after the kiss. Emmeldine finished mixing the herbs, crushing them in her small wooden bowl. She pinched a small mound between her fingers and started rubbing them inside Shaima's lips. Without thinking, she started chanting — a chant she had learned to promote calm and wellbeing to an injured ally.

"*Tutelray alma fosa. Fornasay redba, allamay.*"

Shaima's smile deepened and Emmeldine continued to rub the herbs. After her task was complete, she pulled up a small bench to the bedside and sat as close as she could. She watched the rise and fall of her friend's chest for what felt like moments but was the good part of an entire day. Finally the soft rises stopped, and Shaima's body was still. Emmeldine exhaled the breath she hadn't realized she'd been holding. A single teardrop slid down her cheek and onto the red silk blanket entombing her friend's body. *It is done.*

Chapter 35 - History That Should Not Be Repeated

Emmeldine met briefly with her closest advisors and insisted on a day of rest and mourning before further preparations could be discussed or previous events analyzed. She was exhausted. Her easy life up until recent events, full of personal attention to all her needs, amusements at her request, and constantly pleasant surroundings had not prepared her for this. Yet she was strong.

The thought of possible war, of repeating the mistakes of the past, was terrifying to Emmeldine. She couldn't figure out what else one could do when being attacked. She wished she could ask Shaima her thoughts. If they had more time, it might have been possible to teach defensive magic to enough people to stop the attackers and somehow contain them. But then what? They were not accustomed to capturing such large beings, merely the animal prey upon which they ate. There just wasn't enough time.

Emmeldine left strict instructions with the guards outside her chambers that she was not to be disturbed, and although she missed Tharin's touch, she was deeply relieved to be alone. She slept most of the day and night, rising only to take the trays outside her door and nourish herself. She was *famished*. The next morning she woke feeling wonderfully rested and for a brief moment, before reality came crashing down on her once again, she felt happy.

Just as it all hit her: memories of Shaima's passing, her brother's abduction, her sister's threats, the very likely possibility of war... she heard a knock on the door and she was able to refocus on the present. As she slowly opened it, she saw Daria next to her guards and Tharin standing behind her at a respectful distance.

"My Queen, might we speak privately?" Daria spoke oddly formally in front of the guards and Emmeldine nearly smiled as she gave a quick nod.

Tharin spoke up from across the hall, "I too would like a moment of your time m'lady, when you are done." He gave a courtly bow and Emmeldine rewarded him with a twinkle in her eye as she turned back to her chambers with her friend.

"What say you, Daria? Any news?"

"Nothing new. But I have had some thoughts I would like to share. I worry about too many people knowing about the coming threat. Not only is panic a concern, but also the issues around magic. Perhaps it would be better to evacuate first, claiming a natural disaster? At the very least, I think we should recruit and plan privately... or even continue with your courtship proceedings to cover up what is really underway."

"My goodness! You *have* been thinking. Well, what of my baby sister, Cleo? Have envoys been sent to search for her?"

"We are following up on any previous leads, but it doesn't look good. These are the same leads that were followed before to no avail. Unfortunately, no new information has presented itself in quite some time. We will do what we can."

"I suppose it doesn't really matter. Even if we do find her, I certainly would not hand her over to the likes of Alara!"

"There is that. Perhaps it is best she stay hidden for now, anyway? Assuming she is still alive."

"Yes, assuming that." Emmeldine frowned deeply and shook her head softly.

"I still cannot fathom that she may have been alive and well all this time, that I was denied a life with her in it. If we do find her alive, I hope very much to be a true sister to her, to give her the familial love she has been missing all her days."

"Do you really think Claraceit died several years ago, or was that perhaps a ruse to cover their tracks in hiding your baby sister?"

"This, too, has kept me awake at night. What a deception that would be! And why?"

"I do not know. I'm sorry, Emmeldine — but I really must press you on our current plan. Shall we move forward with the suitors, present as if nothing is amiss? Or evacuate…?"

"No, no, not that. If you think the suitor business will help, then let's go with that. Of course you must realize that choosing a mate is the last thing on my mind right now?"

"Of course I do. I'm not sure I can say the same for the handsome piece of male outside your chamber door!"

"Daria! Goodness! Go with you now, leave me be!" Emmeldine giggled as Daria smiled and walked back out the chamber door. A mere breath later, Tharin's dark head popped in through the entryway, his brown eyes eagerly appraising her.

"Emmeldine! How I have missed you so! Are you well?" His probing eyes assessed her figure and scanned her face as a smile of satisfaction quickly spread across his face when he saw nothing was amiss.

"Goodness Tharin, you act as if something happened since we last spoke! It has barely been more than one eve."

"Aye, well, I missed you. I am so very sorry about Shaima. I know there are things you have not told me that you wished to speak with her about. Might I assume that did not take place?"

Emmeldine shook her head and her eyes started to tear up. She wanted to reach for Tharin for comfort, but given her conversation with Daria, she knew she ought not to.

"No, she had already passed. I'm sorry, but I have matters of the realm I must deal with immediately. I'm afraid I will have to excuse myself."

Tharin's eyes clouded with hurt and Emmeldine felt her heart give a thunk. He slowly turned away.

"As you wish."

Her fists clenched and her jaw tightened as she

pushed the words out of her narrowed lips: "Tharin, there is something you should know. We are moving ahead with my suitors. There will likely be some males visiting the castle shortly. I... thought you should know."

At this, his shoulders slumped and his paced quickened. Giving no verbal indication of having heard her, he simply walked away and quietly shut the door behind him.

Several days later, the palace was a flurry of activity. The halls and common spaces were being prepared for the arrival of Emmeldine's first suitor. Secretly however, preparations were underway for battle. Daria and the other magic users had been dispersed to visit families long-rumored to have magical abilities with the hopes of recruiting as many as possible. The Warriors had also gone off to find strong men and women who were disciplined and respected enough to be of service. Stuck at the palace, Emmeldine tried to keep a calm outward demeanor, while internally she was grieving many things. She knew she had to stay strong and do whatever she could to have a positive outlook, which was challenging in many ways.

Tharin was obviously avoiding her and her heart ached at the thought of causing him pain. Emmeldine knew that now was not the time for romance, and that she could better deceive those around her into believing she was on the verge of choosing a life mate if she did not spend time with him. In the meantime, she received daily updates on the efforts to prepare for Alara's assault. Her usual guards, spies, and other defensive positions were aware of the potential threat but not of the magical nature of it.

Much to Emmeldine's dismay, her suitor arrived right on schedule: Danavin, prince of Galavey.

"My, he is a handsome young male... and with several sisters both older and younger." Ramieda stared with obvious interest of her own as Emmeldine watched him enter the courtyard on a muscular black stallion. She tried to smile.

"His father, the King Husband of Galavey, is known to be a very gentle male who is a good helpmate to his ruling wife, Queen Atricia. Danavin, of course, has been groomed to be similar to his father. He reportedly excels at his studies both academically and emotionally."

Emmeldine nodded. She already knew this information from her briefings, yet still felt a sense of dread at their meeting. He was not Tharin.

Trying to sound pleasant, Emmeldine forced a smile. "Please see that Prince Danavin is given the afternoon to rest and groom before being formally presented at court this evening at the welcome banquet. Make sure he feels warmly welcomed."

"My pleasure, your Majesty. I'm happy to serve."

In the meantime, Emmeldine found herself studying people's features around her quite often, trying to determine who might be of Elven descent. She also wondered whenever she saw someone shorter, broader or darker featured than average if they might be part Dwarven. What other races there might be took over her thoughts as her assistants bored her with talk of preparations for her courtship. She couldn't bear to think about her missing brother, sisters, or potential threats anymore. She tried very hard not to think about Tharin, but she failed. She saw him racing out of the palace temple as she made her way there for her daily prayers to the Goddess. Despite her newly acquired knowledge that the Goddess was not actually their Creator, she had to keep up the pretense of being a devoted Goddess worshiper. There had always been people who do not believe in the Goddess at all, and there were even other deities worshiped in the realm... but Goddess worship had always been the dominant system and was all Emmeldine and her family had ever known. Emmeldine wondered how Tharin would take her news of Shaima's knowledge.

Emmeldine could stall no longer and was led to the banquet room by several of her counsel, including Daria. She saw Elisia waiting near the hall entryway and was both relieved and disappointed to see Tharin was not with her. Emmeldine walked slowly toward the threshold, her long gown flowing behind her in fiery reds, greens and purples. Her hair was piled high in intricate braids and she wore small crystal beads around her hairline. She looked radiant.

Inside the hall, there was barely a square of stone floor without a body standing upon it. The vast room was packed full of onlookers: those eager to see the Queen chose a mate. Emmeldine's council and guards made way for her through the chamber and led her to the high banquet table where Danavin was calmly waiting. Emmeldine took in his fair, fine features and his lean length and decided he most definitely must be of Elven descent, technically a perfect match for her and fit to be King of Trimeria. Disappointment surprised her heart.

"Your Majesty, may I introduce Prince Danavin, third in line as ruler-in-waiting of the lands of Galavey?" The announcer bowed deeply and backed away as Emmeldine graciously nodded her head.

"Prince Danavin, I am humbled by your presence. Your reputation is known far and wide as a wonderful male worthy of any Queen. I thank you for your interest."

"Your Majesty, the pleasure is most assuredly all mine. Thank you for your invitation. I hope you will enjoy our time together." He bowed deeply and looked up at her with clear, wide blue eyes. Emmeldine nodded again and took the hand he extended, letting him help her to their seats. As the courses of steaming, decedent dishes were brought out, Emmeldine smiled widely and laughed loudly, making sure all could see what a wonderful time she was having. She didn't notice when Tharin quietly slipped into the room. She most certainly didn't realize it when he left just as quietly, and quickly.

After the feast there was some fanciful entertainment — music, dancers, and humorous acts. Emmeldine frequently scanned the crowd for Tharin's dark hair and felt a low thump in her heart when he could not be spotted. She found it very difficult to concentrate on the entertainers or her companion, Prince Danavin, who was eager to laugh with her and share light touches. Emmeldine was eager to be done with this event and get her nightly briefing from the leaders of her secret group. Thema and Daria had been whispering together, then both rose quickly and left the banquet, leaving her desperate to know what was going on. Finally, the entertainers completed their show and couples started to amble out of the hall. Emmeldine quickly turned to the prince, who was smiling at her expectantly.

"Thank you, dear Prince for your company this eve. I am sorry to say I am still weary from my recent travels and must bid you goodnight. I hope you shall dine with me on the morrow?"

"Oh what a shame, my dear! Well... thank you, Queen Emmeldine for your most gracious company. I will wait with bated breath for our reunification in the morn. Rest ye well." Danavin bowed deeply and looked at her again with those perfect blue eyes and a beatific smile. *He really is an ideal match for a Queen*, Emmeldine thought, *just not for me.*

As Emmeldine neared her own hall, she saw Daria and Thema waiting for her outside her doorway. She stepped forward to walk toward them, and Tharin stepped out from the shadows. She can smell ale on him and his face held an expression she had never before seen on his usually serene features.

"Emmeldine! Wait, please, I must speak with you." Seeing the guards behind her look at him with alarm, he quickly lowered his voice. "Please."

Emmeldine waved her guards back and held a palm up to signal to Daria all was well, then leaned closer to Tharin and whispered back in a quiet hiss, "Tharin! This is not the time for this! I told you I have to do my duty right now. I can't be seen with you!"

His eyes looked pained, yet he continued with determination, "Aye, I know. But I cannot help how I feel for you. And I know you feel for me too. Please, Emmeldine, let us be together. I know you haven't told me everything that is going on with the ancient arts and your sister but whatever it is, I can face it with you."

"Tharin, please! I cannot make a romantic commitment to you. Not now... and possibly not ever. How can I commit to anyone right now when I don't even know if I will live past next week? My sister and her potential armies pose a great risk to me, to our entire kingdom! I cannot risk distractions of the heart. Please don't push me on this. I would hate to lose you as a friend. "

"As a friend? Is that all I am to you?"

"I value your friendship very much."

His face turns red as his eyes widened then narrowed, his features pushing inward. Wordlessly, he turned on his heel and walked off quickly in the opposite direction. It took every ounce of her will to continue walking toward her chamber door with a serene, untroubled look upon her pale, smooth skin. She joined Daria and Thema and they wordlessly entered her chambers.

As they choose seats near a table set with a map of the realm, Daria tried to catch Emmeldine's eyes and looked at her questioningly. Emmeldine gave a slight shake of her head and glanced at Thema. Now was not the time for the old friends to discuss romance.

"Thank you for joining me in private. As you know, some of my council still does not know we are preparing for battle... but I fear it is time to tell them. Before I make that decision, I want to hear the latest updates so I can be best informed. What say thee?"

Emmeldine's narrowed eyes flashed to Thema, who was studying her intently. She was a successful Warrior who did not miss a thing, having learned long ago to take in all the seemingly small clues to piece together her opponents' next moves.

"Well, your Majesty, of course that will be your decision — but I suggest great caution. There are still those on your council who greatly oppose magic and may turn against you if they think you unwise. That said, we really could use more recruits... and perhaps with the volunteers from their lands to fight, we will have better numbers. It is truly a difficult decision that we must lay at your feet." Thema bows her head. "As for the current situation. There have been no new sightings reported, no hints of openings or magical creatures. A handful of Crones have joined us who seem to have great knowledge of magic and its uses. One of them claims to have been visited by the Fairy folk and had their word they will join us in battle. Unfortunately, this Crone is incredibly elderly and known to hallucinate and talk gibberish, so I'm not so sure how much we can trust her."

Emmeldine, who was smiling at news of the Crones, feels her face fall at the last bit of information. Daria frowned as well, and Thema decided to continue with more positive information.

"The Warriors have recruited a number of fit women who are trained in skills like archery, hunting, athletic excellence and the like. We have started accepting more males since our numbers have not gotten close to our goals as of yet. It is very challenging to recruit while at the same time keeping our purpose very quiet. I hope the use of male fighters does not disturb you, My Queen?"

"No, and why should it? These are desperate times and we can't let old ways hold us back. Somehow, overnight, we have found ourselves in a whole new world."

"But Emmeldine," Daria quickly interjects, "No one

yet knows that the world, our world, has changed. They have no idea."

"They soon will my friend, they soon will."

Chapter 36 - Being Forthright

The next morning, Emmeldine emerged from her council chamber with a pleased smile on her face. *That went much better than I had hoped*! The Queen had stood boldly before her council and calmly explained the course of events of the last few moon cycles. She started with the spies' first report of Alara, then walked them briefly through each event leading up to the current preparations underway. She watched their faces as she spoke and they ranged from shock, surprise, and awe to utter disbelief. All in all, she felt most of her counsel was on her side by the end of the session, and she had little concern that they would be anything but a benefit to her cause. Apparently her father had already spoken to some of the members he had still maintained relationships with after her mother's passing. After he put in some good words for her and gathered their support, he quickly left the palace to go be with his remaining two sons. Once again, Emmeldine felt the love and support of her father cheer her heart. She longed to speak with him about her newfound knowledge, for surely he was as purely bred an Elf as there was left in the lands. She wondered if he could use magic. There had been little mention of males and magic in her learnings.

Several days later, Emmeldine was on her way down to the basements for her daily magic defense training with her core team. After a quick review, the others dispersed to lead training groups elsewhere on the palace grounds, and Emmeldine was left to reluctantly prepare for her day at court. After she cleaned up and re-gowned, she met with her herbalist and procured plant remedies for wounds in cases where magic might possibly fail her. Then she was off to dine with the Prince and his entourage. This is the first part of her day that began to feel unpleasant, and she so wished she could excuse the poor Prince and not put him through the pretenses of a false courtship. She wondered if she should be honest with him, too... but knew it was too risky. She missed Tharin but continued to push him from her mind. If he couldn't be her friend right now, she couldn't make time for him, not even in her thoughts. After sharing an elegant meal with Prince Danavin, Emmeldine received updates in her gathering room about mundane events in her lands. She stifled a yawn as her lands advisor rambled on.

"Crops are coming in nicely, a good harvest of grain this season for sure. Hunters were not as successful this season in the North Woods, and fishing off the coast lands is about the same as always."

Emmeldine frowned at news of hunting trouble. Were the animals scared off or already dead due to magical creatures? What was going on in the North Woods? She mulled this over silently while her assistants asked thoughtful questions of the reporters. Suddenly a trusted spy of hers was admitted to the chamber by her guard outside. She sat up quickly and felt her heart leap. This spy, who went by Grenecia on palace grounds, only ever showed up if something of great import to the Queen had occurred. Which, until recently, had been very rare indeed.

"Clear the room, please, everyone. I must speak with Grenecia alone."

The five women and two men present quickly cleared and left her alone with her most trusted source of information.

"As always Grenecia, I invite you to speak freely."

The petite woman bowed her head and looked up with clear brown eyes that reminded the Queen of someone she was desperately trying not to think of.

"Your Majesty. I am here to tell you that two members of your council are attempting to raise others against you. They say that you speak heresy against the Goddess and are convincing others that magic is real. There are quite a few who are upset at this news and are starting to question your mind. That is all." Grenecia looked down and kept her head bent respectfully.

"Goodness! Well that *is* quite a lot, isn't it? Whom might these two council members be?" Emmeldine heard the names in her own head before Grenecia could open her mouth.

"Maena and Nathalya. They often opposed your mother and have always been... let us say... *particular.*"

Emmeldine silently nodded. She stood behind the table and thought for a few moments, then looked back into the spy's calm brown eyes and sighed.

"I need you to go to the North Woods — find out why the hunting season has been so poor there."

"Whatever you wish, My Queen. I will make haste." Grenecia turned and left the chambers quickly.

Emmeldine sat down heavily in her chair and put her hands up to her head, rubbing gently. She knew this day would come, where her usually peaceful palace would be filled with division, yet she had so hoped that day could be put off till the last possible moment. It seemed fate had other things in store. She tried to think strategically, to fight off the shred of doom trying to crawl into her heart. Emmeldine knew there were far worse things coming her way then her own people turning against her. Although once, not too long ago, that would have been the worst outcome she could imagine.

She decided she must speak to her naysayers directly, with the support of some of her team that could also serve as witnesses to recent magic events. She was just about to summon Daria and Thema back when there was a brisk knock at her door. She opened it quickly.

A female guard with a pained expression on her face spoke rapidly: "My Queen, Prince Danavin is having his people pack his things to leave. They are loading the horses as we speak!"

"What? How can this be? Did something hap... Oh, oh I see. Send for Maena and Nathalya at once, I will take no excuses for their absence. And send someone to Danavin and ask him to please wait for me, that I would very much like to speak to him before he departs. Hurry!"

She sat down heavily on a stool by the table and took some deep breaths. Emmeldine wished more than ever that the Goddess really was their creator so she could pray to her right now. She suddenly felt very alone. There was another knock at her door, this time very gentle. She stood to open it and before she could take a step, it started to open... and Tharin's warm smile shone back at her. Without a word, she stepped into his arms and he held her tight. While she basked in the comfort, she still had the clarity of thought to wonder how he always seemed to show up just when she needed him most. She decided it must be good fortune.

"I saw Danavin preparing to leave, quite hastily I might add. I am so happy of this, dear Emmeldine. I hope..."

"Tharin, please, please stop. Just hold me tight, might you?" She looked up at him with wide eyes brimming with tears, and he instantly closed his mouth and squeezed her a little tighter.

After a few minutes of this peaceful reprieve, there was a solid knock at the door, and Tharin quickly let go of Emmeldine and took a few steps away from her toward the other side of the table. Emmeldine smoothed her gown and spoke calmly.

"You may enter."

She remained standing and gestured for Nathalya and Maena to sit down with a simple wave of the hand and a solemn face. They did so quickly. She also motioned for the guards to stay.

"I hear you have some disagreements with me? I take it this has led to our beloved prince Danavin preparing for departure? What say you?"

"My Queen, with due respect. Magic use and Goddess heresy are against the basic tenets of the realm. As soon as we learned you did not worship the Goddess, and in fact were attempting to use magic despite its evil nature, we felt it our duty to warn the poor Prince before he was caught in a heretical marriage." Nathalya spoke for them both; Maena merely stared at the floor near her feet and grasped her hands before her. Both sets of eyes flickered toward Tharin questioningly.

"I see. Do you not believe that my mother and her mother before her were ordained by the very Goddess you speak of, that I am indeed the rightful heir to this throne?"

"Those things are true."

"Do you not believe as I am the rightful Queen and you my subject, that you should trust in my wisdom and allow me the freedom to make the decisions I think best?"

"Again, your Majesty, with due respect, heresy against the Goddess is never allowable, not even by the Queen."

"I see. And what pray tell do you intend to do about it?"

"We are preparing a statement to present to the council. We will also be talking to the committee of elders and asking their advice. Currently several solutions are under consideration. I'd rather not say more than that."

"Indeed! And why should I not have you detained right now? You are plotting against the Queen!"

"Your Majesty, we are not plotting. Merely aspiring to make sure our realm continues to be run in a just and pure way as it has since its conception. We have the right to inquire and to inform. We are doing nothing wrong."

"Aspiring is a good word to describe your intentions. The question is, what are you aspiring to do? What do you think will happen if my rule is questioned? There is not yet an heir; do you really want a Queendom with no Queen?" Emmeldine could hear her voice becoming shrill and just managed to stop herself before saying something she might regret.

Maena and Nathalya were working hard to keep their expressions blank. Emmeldine had the impression that they had been prepared for this moment... but she had no idea how or why.

"Listen to me. I am the Queen. I have broken no laws of this land. There is an imminent threat approaching, and I am doing everything in my power to prepare to protect our people. It is a personal decision and not decreed by law who one worships. It is none of your business whether I believe in the Goddess or not. As a people we have historically been Goddess worshipers. Perhaps that will change — perhaps it will not. Time will tell. In the meantime, I suggest you align yourself with me, if you value the lives of your friends and families. If you value the homes you have come to make...align yourself with me."

The two chastised council members exchanged quick looks and gave small nods. Maena finally spoke up, "If we may, your Majesty, we would like to return to our own lands now to gather fighters and see our families secured."

"I will allow it. I certainly hope that is all you will be doing."

With nods and shallow bows the two women quickly left. Tharin jumped up immediately and hurried over to her.

"You mustn't trust them, Emmeldine! I have heard them speak ill of you before; they are not your friends!"

"Yes, I agree. I want them followed to their homes, and I want reports back immediately of their interactions. Can you oversee this yourself?"

"Of course! Anything for you." With a quick kiss on the cheek, Tharin turned and left the room hastily. Emmeldine sighed deeply and felt slightly reassured that at least Tharin would be occupied and out of harm's way for a few days. That gave her some comfort. Now she had to try and keep Danavin at court lest more suspicions be aroused — a task she was not looking forward to.

Late in the eve as the sky darkened to its final hue of an inky bluish-black, Emmeldine was able to retire to her chambers to rest. Danavin had been convinced to stay, they had dined royally for all to see, and Tharin was well on his way to see what her wayward council members were up to. Emmeldine fell asleep that night succumbing to an old ritual she found hard to let go of: she prayed to the Goddess. She prayed for guidance and peace, and she prayed for the conflicts she was faced with to be ended without bloodshed. Several tears sat on her cheek as she fell asleep, symbols of the inevitability of her prayers falling on silent ears.

Chapter 37 - At Last

Emmeldine usually woke of her own accord slightly after dawn. Several days after she had sent Grenecia to the North, she was awoken unexpectedly in the dark of night. Startled, she blinked rapidly while trying to pull herself from her dream state. She had been in a lovely meadow, Tharin had been there, and everything had been peaceful and calm. Suddenly, she was awake and staring up into the very serious face of Grenecia.

"Your Grace, I am so sorry! You must awaken, there may not be much time."

"What? How did you…. something happened?" Emmeldine rubbed at her eyes and tried to pull herself into reality. Tharin and the meadow beckoned tauntingly.

"Yes. Your grace, are you awake? Take a moment." Grenecia watched her young Queen with concern and waited until she was sure her eyes were clear and attentive.

"Alara was spotted to the North! I saw her from a distance myself. She had magical creatures with her for sure. There were beasts of the like I have never seen in our lands — dark hooded beings with foul stench, furry beasts, creatures I could not have imagined. It was a terrible sight. They appeared to be resting at the time, but presumably they are marching this direction at this very moment! You must put the castle on high alert!"

"So it is happening at last. I shall be reunited with my sister… in war." Emmeldine shivered and started to lift her covers to get out of her bed. Grenecia helped her into her thick robes and she stood on shaky legs in the middle of the bedchamber.

"At last. We shall resolve this, one way or another." Emmeldine's eyes hardened and she set her jaw.

"Yes, I dare say we shall. I am here to fight. The sight and scent of those creatures was enough to convince me: this is a cause worth fighting for. Dying for, I dare say. I am at your service."

Emmeldine suddenly felt clear headed and as awake as she had ever been.

"Yes — I think you're right, Grenecia. Whether we live or die, this is the right thing to do."

Emmeldine quickly dressed in her leathers, grabbed a few items she had prepared, and left her chambers... possibly for the last time. She made sure to wrap her mother's wooden beads around her wrist as she hastily exited.

"Grenecia, wake all my ladies and council members and tell them it is time. Ask them to bring their gear and meet in the courtyard immediately."

Grenecia turned briskly and headed off toward her task at a rapid pace.

Emmeldine had already decided to meet the onslaught away from the palace if possible, to spare the innocents of what was to come. She gathered her supporters quietly in the courtyard, and they spread out to find their own recruits. They arranged a meeting spot outside of the surrounding towns with the promise to meet up by early sun. The thought of sending for Tharin, of having his comforting gaze upon her as they rode off was tempting, yet she knew she should not put his life at risk. Tharin was no Warrior, no Mage, and surely his only outcome in battle would be death. Emmeldine could not bear to think of it. So she rode off without him, but alongside the many strong females she had come to care for and the males they had trained.

Emmeldine fought to keep her mind on the battle plans as they rode hard. She could not afford the distracting thoughts of Damin, Tharin, Shaima's absence, or the many other things that had been weighing on her heart of late. She couldn't help but think, however, of her baby sister Cleo whom Alara had demanded the presence of. Would she really hold their brother captive forever if Emmeldine could not produce their baby sister? Emmeldine still had no leads as to the young girl's whereabouts... and for all she knew Cleo was truly dead.

As they neared the meeting point, Emmeldine felt a pang of relief as she saw many riders flowing into the valley, followed by line after line of others on foot. She had been quite concerned their recruitment would be inadequate given the short timeframe and need for secrecy, but it appeared they had fared better than she could have hoped. She saw a large horse-drawn carriage carrying six elderly females, and she guessed they were the Crones she had heard of. She hoped their advanced knowledge would save lives and prevent bloodshed, especially their own. It suddenly hit Emmeldine how she was asking all these good people to risk their own lives... for *her*. She almost couldn't breathe as she felt the weight of it. Yet she knew she had no other choice.

As eyes turned to her for direction, Emmeldine stood tall and used the strongest voice she could despite the chill in her throat: "We must fan out to lead other sections of fighters. Make sure to spread the magic users evenly to ensure some level of protection. Once a section is formed and the leaders have some sense of order, file out. Head north." Her throat tightened and she bit her cheeks. Surprise clenched her softly as those around her headed off, following her direction. *What am I doing?* Emmeldine was uncertain whether to go ahead and lead the charge, or to stay back and see to everyone's well departure. As the first group crested the hills before her, she decided to ask Daria to stay back to see all proceeded well.

Emmeldine raced her trusty mare hard, glad he had been rested and pampered for many days now. Not quite as many as she had planned, though. She didn't know why she was surprised at Alara's showing up before the two fortnights she had offered. There was no reason to expect her sister to be an honest woman. However, in spite of all that had occurred and all that threatened to come, Emmeldine still felt love in her heart for the little girl who used to follow her down the palace halls, hair bouncing and skirts flapping as they raced and played. Every time she thought of it, her heart began to break anew. She desperately hoped that when the time came, with her sister staring at her hatefully and ordering beasts to tear her asunder, that she would have the strength to do what needed to be done to stop her.

They rode hard, reaching their intended camp destination shortly before nightfall. Scouts approached her as small tents were quickly erected..

"My Queen! Alara's forces are a few hours' ride north and appear to be making camp themselves."

"And what of their number?"

"I do not believe there are as many bodies coming this way as are currently present in the surrounding camps. Admittedly though, we were not able to get close enough to safely examine the beings... and some appeared rather large from a distance. We were able to hear shrieks and hisses from afar that sounded quite numerous, and the creatures were quite unpleasant in appearance and smell, to say the least."

"Thank you. Please arrange for a night watch a safe distance away. We certainly do not want to be awakened by such wretched beasts!" She shivered and turned toward the sound of Daria approaching from the back of the campsite. The women stepped into each other's arms and embraced tightly.

"Daria! Am I ever glad to see you! All is well, everyone accounted for?"

"As far as we know. We have never experienced group movement like this before. The Warriors have been very helpful, though. I think all is well." She wiped her dirt-smeared face and smiled at her royal friend encouragingly.

"Thank you! It feels ever so much better with you here. I only wish there wasn't the issue of Cleoandra. There is no telling how Alara will react to her absence. It's so ridiculous and unfair." Her cheeks blazing with heat, she breathed deeply as Daria gently squeezed her hand.

"It's all unfair, my dear — *all* of it. Yet... here we are. Let's get some rest." Emmeldine consulted with one of her top Warriors about defensive strategy for the eve and confirmed with her present Council members that there continued to be no sign of Cleo. There had been so much going on, and they were moving so quickly that Emmeldine feared she had missed something important. Some angle or idea that would help ensure success. Finally, when the night deepened to its silkiest black, she fell into a light, fitful slumber.

The first thing she was conscious of hearing was soft coughs, the rustle of stones and leaves being brushed aside by moving bodies, and anxious whispers of anticipation around her.

"Do you think they all have claws and fangs?"

"I hear some can shoot you down with their thoughts."

"Surely we have some weapons or sorcery that are stronger?

The next thing she noticed were the scents. There was a tangy hint of fresh dew mixed with a moldy dirt smell. The faint odor of wood fire clung to the early morning air. Emmeldine inhaled deeply and slowly opened her eyes. The sky was cloudy, a dark, murky grey that threatened rain yet felt oddly flat. Definitely befitting a day no one present looked toward with anything but dread.

Those around her instantly quieted as they saw their Queen rise from having slept on a simple floor mat, same as them. They seemed confused about whether to nod or bow or to look away in respect. Emmeldine decided to make things easy for them all and walked away to find her primary group of magic users. Daria, Chloe and Marianee were all nearby talking quietly amongst themselves.

"Good morn, your Majesty. We are ready to face the day with ya. I was just telling Daria that it be best to stand our ground near here, maybe to the north on the hillside.

Give us a sight advantage. Then we can best prepare the proper spell or strategy based on what be coming."

"Honestly Chloe, I will have to take your advice on this. I have no idea about the ways of war, no concept of how to be successful. I only know the magic we have learned and practiced as a team and what I learned through my private studies with Shaima. I hope that is enough."

Chloe and Daria nodded their heads encouragingly, and Marianee offered one of her rare beatific smiles. "Of course, your Majesty. We shall prevail!"

"I'm glad you…"

"Where is the Queen?" A frantic cry called out and a tall figure came racing forward. It was a Warrior woman in tight leathers with two thin swords tied across her back. "Your Majesty! Thank the Goddess I found you. They are closing in! I'd guess about a few thousand strands from here by now."

"All right then, this is it! Chloe, shall we fall forward and see if we can still get the hillside advantage?" Emmeldine stood tall and looked her people straight in the eyes. Now was the time to lead bravely, and she did not want to let them down.

"We have to hurry — quick as can be. Let's go!" Chloe lunged forward.

They quickly fell into their marching formations from the day before, mounting horses and leaving unnecessary supplies behind. Soon they were riding out toward a hostile force...one they had only begun to understand.

Chapter 38 - This Is Not The End

They smelled them long before they could see them. At first, tiny infrequent whiffs of foul stench were in the air. Slowly the stench began to linger, and long before the first sighting, noses were permanently wrinkled in disgust. Emmeldine and her team were no longer disturbed by the smell, having experienced it so many times before. A similar assault on their ears slowly built as they neared. A cacophony of grunts, groans, hisses and yelps warned them of impending doom. Emmeldine experienced a familiar sensation she first felt during her first magical encounter in the palace basements, a sinking of spirit that she struggled to describe. It was almost as if the magical creatures approaching were taking her energy from afar. It was a faint feeling, but she deeply feared what would happen if it increased as they neared. She started her chant of protection and felt an immediate surge within herself. She had fought it off, whatever it was.

Finally, they appeared. Emmeldine saw a figure at the lead, dressed royally in dark purple riding clothes and carrying a sword.

"I wonder if my sister has taken to studying the defensive arts while she was gone, or if she plans to rely on magic herself?" While her musings were directed toward her nearest companions Chloe and Ramieda, she was not surprised when the only answer was the soft fall of their footsteps on the moist earth. Emmeldine motioned for those who could view her to stop, and the message quickly rippled outward. They were looking downhill at the approaching legion, and from what Emmeldine could see, their number was larger then she had hoped — but not impossibly so. They were coming out of a narrow, forested valley surrounded by hills and towering mountains. There was little plant life between them, a few trees and bushes scattered about, a small stream with rocky shores. Nowhere to hide.

The defensive group led by the Queen was on a grassy hillside above the valley. They had recently come through some sparse woods and were mostly standing in a large meadow which sat between the woods and the rocky valley below.

"So still it be, no bird calls here. Nothing moves," Chloe observed, giving voice to Emmeldine's thoughts.

The birds had indeed gone completely silent and the wind itself seemed to suddenly disappear. They were all trying very hard to be brave given the unnatural nature of the entire endeavour, and once again, Emmeldine was overtaken with the thought of not wanting to let them down. They must prevail.

Emmeldine saw Alara step forward, and it looked as if she was trying to shout something up the hillside at her. Emmeldine could not make out any words from that distance. Suddenly she saw another figure step up beside her sister, someone tall and draped in a black cloak. The figure put its hand on Alara's shoulder, and suddenly her voice was amplified. As the first words hit Emmeldine, she took a step back and flinched. It was uncanny in many ways to have her sister's voice thrust into her ears after so many years.

"This is your only chance to be shown mercy. Give me my baby sister at once and I will release your useless brother. Otherwise, no one shall be spared and I will take what's mine."

Emmeldine flinched again and the thought flashed through her mind of how odd it was that Alara considered their sister hers but their brother solely Emmeldine's. She shook her head and felt her heart give a tug. This was it, then. She tried to think of a way to amplify her own voice, but lacking knowledge of a suitable spell, she was unable. She simply cupped her hands to her mouth and did her best to project down the hillside.

"I could not find her. I do not know if she lives.

Please, please release Damin! He is just a boy and has nothing to do with your discontent. I beseech you, Alara!"

Alara stood still below as if in thought, then the hooded figure leaned over to whisper in her ear. Suddenly, Alara raised her sword and shouted out. The swarm of creatures and magical folk behind her let out a cheer that sounded more like anguished excitement. They surged forward. The more recognizable creatures that resembled beasts of Trimeria quickly took the lead: feline and canine nightmares. Lumbering behind them were a dozen or so tall, thick, incredibly muscular beings who moved very slowly. Emmeldine felt the word "Ogre" buzz in her head. Beneath them, she thought she spotted some of the creatures such as the one she and Shaima had encountered in the palace dungeons. There were also beings headed their way that had features of several different life forms. Emmeldine did not have time to even guess what they could be.

As the furry beasts came close to cresting the hilltop, Emmeldine and the other magic users raised their hands and shot white light at them. All but one of the first line of creatures fell and that beast, a feline, jumped high and landed on one of the recruited fighters. Luckily, an experienced Warrior was nearby and slayed the beast quickly, but the fighter was heavily wounded and was led away from the frontline. After that, there was an onslaught. Creatures and beings became intermeshed, white light shot in various directions, chants and spells shouted and whispered, smoke, and soon a kaleidoscope of colorful lights streaking like lightning through the hills.

Emmeldine made sure to stay near the Warriors and magic users she knew closely — together they were a powerful force in fighting back the offense. During a quick moment when no threat was near, she looked around to find her sister and could not manage to lay eyes on her. The sky was becoming hazy around them, but as she looked down the hillside, she saw many more magical creatures headed their way. Her heart sank. She wasn't sure how much longer her people could prevail. Especially those less trained.

"Watch out!" Chloe cried as Emmeldine felt a coldness touch her backside. Emmeldine spun around and saw an Ogre and two Goblins headed straight toward her. Quickly, she thought of a powerful wall protecting her and thrust up her hands. The white light shot out forcefully and she almost fell backward but was caught by Ramieda, who had rushed over at Chloe's call.

"I've got you."

Suddenly, the wall of white started to push back as the creatures resist. *I'm not strong enough!*

"You both must join me, touch my arm!"

Like a flash, the women joined together and the white light pulsed powerfully. The advancing creatures dropped to the ground and were still.

"There is another group about to crest the hill. Ready yourselves!" the head archer yelled.

"Ramieda and Chloe, let's not be parted. As soon as the archers back off we shall advance!" Emmeldine breathlessly knelt to rest momentarily. Looking around frantically, she was reassured to see Marianee, Daria, and Sarsha off to the west side of the hills, physically united with white light pouring out of them toward the approaching beasts of magic.

The new group of magical creatures were almost up the hill and the archers raised their bows. Right as the head archer started to raise her hand for the release signal, there was a near-deafening crash coming from the hill to the east. Emmeldine felt the ground beneath her feet begin to shake. Her cry was joined by a chorus of others as they suddenly fell to the ground. Violent rumbling and loud sounds of falling rock and earth shifting against itself intensified and Emmeldine was forced to cover her ears. She looked up and cried out again upon seeing a split in the earth to the east of them. The ground slowly opened further, like the mouth of an expectant predator hiding in the brush. Rich brown soil fell heavily, and emerald mosses and plants tore away easily.

Below, a gaping emptiness of black air hung forebodingly.

By the time her eyes could take it all in, everything around them froze. There was dust from the upturned earth floating every which way, but besides that, not a creature nor being moved on either side. Just as several sets of eyes started to turn from the opened ground back to the battlefield, the vast expanse of open earth suddenly exploded with color. Tiny bright bursts came flying out toward Alara's forces. Blues, greens, reds, yellows and more. Colors this realm had no words for. Hues separated and enlarged, starting first as small orbs, then growing quickly to the size of a full-grown being. These beings started shooting their colorful light at the invaders, who then started to fall to the ground or disappear altogether. Emmeldine watched in awe, her heart soaring with hope. The Fairies had arrived!

"Emmeldine!"

Suddenly she felt a tug on her arm and saw Ramieda point toward the crest of the hill they stood on. Several large Ogres were nearing them. Their stench was almost as foul as their features. They stood taller and wider then any being from this realm. Large eyes oozed fluid and hard black pupils swung wildly in their orbs. Hair sprouted randomly all over their heads and bodies in large erratic patches. Large hands and feet were thick with long, dirty nails that looked like claws. When they opened their mouths to moan and scream, Emmeldine saw row upon row of sharp teeth. She shivered. Without words, the two women joined hands and raised them toward the creatures. Chloe quickly joined them after shouting some directions toward the archers.

In unison, so as to give their words more power, they recited the spell they had practiced to take down such creatures. Several Warriors stood nearby with spears and arrows ready.

"*Do Mei Letarr Tomee baa.*"

The first foul foe fell, but the second picked up speed and swung at the closest Warrior, knocking her down to the ground with an audible *smack*. Emmeldine momentarily lost her concentration as she cried out and turned toward the fallen figure. Chloe reached out to stop her and gestured for them to refocus on the Ogre that was now only barely out of reach. The Warriors were throwing spears and shooting arrows rapidly, but they bounced off the creature or were swatted away as if nothing more then flying insects. This time, when the three women proceeded to wield their magic, their voices were forceful, strong, and more determined than ever.

"Do Mei Letarr Tomee baa. Do Mee Letarr Tomee baa!"

The white light shone fiercely and thrust itself at the putrid Ogre, stopping it in its tracks a mere rock's throw from where they stood. Emmeldine noticed its eyebrows lift in surprise just before it fell, and saw sprays of spittle and other wretched fluids surrounding the creature as it tumbled. The earth shook.

Ramieda squeezed her hand reassuringly, then let go and took a step forward.

"An abomination for sure, foul creature." She shook her head and spit toward the fallen form.

Daria raced up to them. "Look! The Fairies are beating them back! It looks like hardly any of our foes remain!" Her curls were tied back, but her head bobbed just the same. She pointed downhill at the retreating creatures and beings that were being swiftly pursued by colorful flying figures.

"My goodness, the Fairies really did come to our aid. Although, they did say they could not stay in our realm long, and …" Emmeldine's eyes enlarged and her mouth opened slightly as she trailed off. Alarmed, Daria turned from her friend and looked down the hill once again.

"Goddess, no!"

The lights were shrinking rapidly. Those that had chased creatures off disappeared into the distance, and those that remained closer visibly shrank until they had all but disappeared. Then, they did.

"Oh no! They're gone!" Emmeldine quickly scanned

the surrounding landscape and breathed a sigh of relief. It appeared that almost all the foes were gone, either fled or destroyed. "My friends, look — I think we might have won!"

The women scanned the scene and saw the Crones fighting a remaining troll down the hill; they had it cornered and apparently under control. There were several other magic fighters containing a small group of magical beasts just below them. In the distance, they could see a group of black hooded figures entering the woods, then disappearing from sight. The four women shivered unknowingly. Suddenly, Emmeldine caught sight of a brilliant purple figure stepping out of the woods and looking straight up at the hill. Right at where Emmeldine stood. Alara.

She heard Daria gasp and felt others come closer, as if a swarm were protecting its Queen. Emmeldine's heart raced and her breathing slowed all at once. Everything began to feel unreal. The air tauntingly brushed against her skin as it playfully blew around them, almost teasingly. The sounds she heard were muted and muffled, as if her head were covered with cloth. She knew several people were trying to direct her, to give her advice on her next moves. All that Emmeldine could hear was her own heart thumping and the slow whoosh of breath that occasionally escaped her mouth. Her eyes remained fixed on Alara, who was now approaching the bottom of the hillside. She momentarily disappeared from sight as she reached the bottom, then reappeared and slowly began to ascend. Emmeldine realized her archers were loading their arrows, and she quickly moved to stop them.

"Wait! No! Let me try to talk to her first." Suddenly her whole body came alive and she felt flushed with heat. Emmeldine rushed to a better vantage point and saw her sister frozen in her tracks when she saw the archers. Alara looked up at her, green eyes blazing.

"Where is my baby sister? I want her at once! I will release Damin when I have her. He is of no use to me." Alara gestured to the woods behind her and Emmeldine saw several of the dark figures emerge, holding an almost grown boy. She could not tell from that far away whether he was her brother, but the height and coloring appeared similar. Emmeldine was troubled by these dark figures. *Who are they?*

"Alara! Sister, please. Let us talk face to face, just you and I." Emmeldine leaned over the rocky ledge and saw Alara nod her head in consent. Emmeldine stepped over to a worn path down the hill and slowly made her way over to her sister. Each footfall felt heavy as she frantically tried to think how she could convince her sister to leave peacefully and give custody of their brother to her. She tried to keep her face neutral and her stance strong without appearing threatening. Emmeldine pinched several of the fingers on her right hand together to let out some of the tension that threatened to burst out of her body. The sting helped her clear her mind.

When she got to within a stone's throw of her younger sister, she stopped. Alara had grown taller since she had seen her years ago; she now looked about equal in height to her sister, the Queen. Her golden hair was braided back tightly — small rows woven into one long rope that rested heavily between her shoulder blades. Her green eyes were as large and intense as Emmeldine remembered. Her bronze-hued skin that resembled her kin from the Northland was now richer than before, as if Alara had spent much time outdoors. Her body, too, had thickened and appeared well-muscled — long, strong limbs shot out of her curvy frame. Her beautiful features quickly turned ugly as she snarled at Emmeldine.

"Do you have her or not? I want her now!"

"Alara, I don't even know if she is alive. Last I heard, she died as a baby. I've had people looking, but…"

"You lie!"

Alara raced at Emmeldine and tackled her to the ground. The wood beads started to glow against Emmeldine's chest after freeing themselves from her tunic. Alara stared at them with alarm. Emmeldine pushed back and had almost forced her way out of Alara's grasp when she heard a low howl. The sound intensified, and she felt a strong wind hit her body. As the pressure of the gale grew stronger yet, Emmeldine realized her entire body was being forced down by the air. She fought with all her might but could not move. She looked at Alara who had backed a few feet away and she appeared untouched...only a few wisps of escaped hair gently swaying against her face.

Emmeldine gasped as the wind battered against her, the feeling of losing control of her body chilling her to the core. The gust got so strong she felt as if her limbs might tear right off, and she could barely breathe for all the air knocking around her head. The glowing beads started to radiate a white light towards Alara, then bursts of white started shooting towards the retreating princess. Emmeldine felt like she was about to faint when suddenly... it stopped. The beads sat calmly against her chest, appearing wooden once again. All was still.

She looked to Alara and saw her still standing close by, but now her radiant skin had gone sallow and her eyes had turned to the lands below. Her entire body appeared to tremble slightly as she opened her mouth to speak.

"Father? Is that really you?"

Regaining control of her body, Emmeldine strained to see what Alara's gaze had found. A male was walking toward them rapidly. The Queen's eyes lifted in shock as she takes in the personage. Dono.

Chapter 39 - To Not Believe

"Alara! What is this I hear of you causing harm to your sister? Our Queen? Please be it to the Goddess this isn't true. Come here, Daughter!"

Emmeldine watched in awe as her sister walked away from her and went down the hill to her father. She quickly glanced to the woods and saw the dark figures retreat once again, this time without the boy. She started to race toward him, scrambling down the rocky banks to avoid the path Dono and Alara were now embracing on. Emmeldine heard snippets of the conversation as she went down.

"No father, of course there is no magic. I was simply…"

"Mustn't shame me…"

Now Emmeldine understood why the cloaked beings had disappeared. As she looked around, she noticed that all signs of magical creatures had disappeared, almost as if nothing had ever happened. The dead beasts, Ogres, and other creatures were all gone. Her fighters that had been injured remained and were now being attended to by others. She knew there were some dead, but they were currently out of her sight. Shaking her head, she kept her eyes on Damin and raced up to him. She squealed in joy.

"Oh, my baby brother! I am ever so happy to see you well! Are you well?"

"Aye sister, Emmeldine, uh… My Queen?" He looked confused, as if trying to decide whether to bow or embrace her. She solved it for him and quickly swept him up into her arms. Damin had grown into a lanky young male, and she gazed at him adoringly at the conclusion of their embrace. Her brothers features were fair like hers: elegant, pointy ears and a lean frame. His hair was much lighter than her deep red, a pale hue that was charming on a young lad. Eyes were blue as well, but more a mild sky blue than her brilliant sapphires. His grin was wide and warm, a face full of love.

"I am ever so relieved! I knew you would save me, but our sister Alara, she could be quite the intimidator, she could! I was worried once or twice I must admit. And her friends…"

"Oh, brother! I am so sorry. And I have so much to ask you. First we must ensure your well-being and care for your body. Then later, when all is well, we shall talk and talk. I assure you, I want nothing more."

"That sound marvelous Emmel… uh, My Queen?"

"Nonsense! Call me sister, or Emmeldine as you see fit. We are family!" She smiled lovingly at him and then eagerly looked to where she had last seen Alara and Dono. She was worried Alara might still attack, and still unsure of Dono's position in all of this. Surely he had known his daughter's whereabouts… or had he?

Alara and Dono had walked quite far away in the few moments since she had greeted her brother. Alara's back was retreating into the tree line, and Dono had turned around and was quickly walking back toward Emmeldine. She felt bodies lining up behind her and knew Daria and the Warriors were near.

"Queen Emmeldine, please, *please* forgive my daughter. I have been traveling these last seasons and she has never recovered from her grief over your mother's death. I'm sad to say she has suffered quite a lot. Her mind… well, she has quite the imagination and doesn't always see things clearly. I do apologize if she has done any harm. I thought when I left her in her own estate she inherited from your mother that she would find joy in running her own lands. Foolishly, I thought the responsibility and freedom would heal her. I must get her back to my own home now… if you please, your Majesty? I promise to keep her there until such time as she gets better. I pray to the Goddess every day for her recovery and I do believe she shall have it. May we beg your leave?"

Dono looked up at her solemnly, and Emmeldine knew in that moment that he had truly no idea who his daughter really was or what she was capable of. Still, she thought if he was volunteering to be her captor, it was certainly an option she should consider. She thought of her mother and the love this male had shown her, and knew she wanted to spare him further grief if she could.

"Dono, I know you are a good male. If you pledge your word that my sister Alara will remain confined in your ancestral village, that you will personally ensure that she does not leave again without my permission, then yes, you may both go now."

"I do. I will, your Majesty Emmeldine — thank you."

Emmeldine opened her mouth to speak then paused, her words unable to exit. She wanted to speak to Alara, to somehow get reassurance of peace from her herself... and at the same time, forge a truce of sisterhood. Instead, she slowly closed her lips and sighed silently.

Dono's wrinkled brown eyes slightly watered and he bowed his greying head. He slowly backed away a few steps, then turning and standing tall, walked away. Back to the woods.

Chapter 40 - Falling Action

It was past midday by the time Emmeldine had said goodbye to Dono. She was filled with so many thoughts: Alara, Dono, the return of her brother... and most troubling, the cloaked figures that seemed to be empowering her sister somehow. The sight of the injured and knowledge of probable deaths cut her to the core. When she looked around and saw the evidence of devastation from the magical battle that had suddenly disappeared, she ached and started to shake uncontrollably. The physical manifestation of shock intensified to the point that she had to ask several Warriors to construct a makeshift shelter for her to rest in. As soon as her body stilled, she invited her advisors in to decide on next steps.

"It is safe to head back to the palace in the morning. A fully armed guard will take shifts in the night, and with Alara heading back to Dono's lands, there should be little chance of threat." Ramieda bowed her head as the silent space filled with shifting bodies and throats clearing. It bothered Emmeldine that Alara showed no ability to access magic herself... well, with the possible exception of the winds. She thought back to the day in the gardens when she thought she had heard Alara talking to the Crone. The memory was still confusing, but made more sense now then before. Perhaps Alara had the power of the air? What really concerned Emmeldine were the cloaked figures. Who were they, and where did they come from? She felt a deep sense of unease whenever she thought of them.

Sarsha and Marianee were seeing to the Crones and other groups that needed care. Daria, Chloe, Ramieda, and Thema sat with her as her most trusted advisors.

"I know any death be tragic my dears, yet I am glad to say there are only a dozen or so for sure, yet more injured. Not the best outcome for us all, though might a' been much worse. Let us thank the Goddess...er, well, thank goodness anyway!" Chloe slumped in her seated position, her usual bounce lost in exhaustion.

Suddenly Damin's voice was outside the tent, clear as day. He was laughing and expressing gratitude to someone assisting him in gathering food and bedding. Emmeldine's heart flushed with relief at his safety, and a huge smile spread across her weary features. The others looked at her quizzically, and she reminded herself that her hearing seemed to be abnormally good. Not something she wanted to draw attention to in this moment.

"I was thinking of my brother. I am ever so relieved he is well, and so grateful for all everyone has done to ensure so. While the cost has been high, I know we have done what we must to defend the realm and retrieve the prince."

"Aye!"

"Here, here!"

The gathered women smiled back at their friend and ruler. Thema stood and faced her Queen.

"Luckily, our location is very remote. We are all but certain that no one outside of the opposing groups knew of the magic used or saw anything."

Emmeldine was dragged back into strategic planning and let her brother's voice fade from her thoughts.

Thema continued, "We have two spies and a Warrior following Dono and Alara back to his lands. We will get regular reports of their whereabouts and activities from now on."

Thema cleared her throat and looked down, and Emmeldine realized there was something she wanted to say but was struggling with.

"Yes? There is more to that?"

"Well, your Majesty, with respect... I must say that I feel it is a mistake to let them roam wild. Alara intentionally tried to harm you and kidnapped your brother. She is unpredictable and unsafe. She should not be free."

"I understand your concerns, Thema — and I am sure

most people that were here today think the same. There is a lot to consider. Capturing her would bring a lot of attention to our recent activities and would reveal magic to the people at large. This would also hurt Dono and possibly endanger him... and I do believe he is innocent. If she is imprisoned, her magical allies might seek to free her — but if she is simply detained by her own father, I am hoping to avoid further attack. And, well... there is the fact that she *is* my sister, and I wish her no harm."

Emmeldine brushed away a tear and tried to smile.

"Today was a victorious day! We were able to defend ourselves adequately and the Fairies are clearly our allies, and strong allies at that. My brother is safe and well! Please, might we revel in the good outcomes of the day for now and strategize about possible foes on the morrow?"

Thema and the others nodded and smiled. Tomorrow would come soon enough.

The rhythmic clacking of the horses' hooves on the uneven ground was filled with just enough unpredictability to mirror their riders' flurry of emotions. Smiling eagerly at Damin, Emmeldine felt her heart beat faster as she took in his merry face. What a happy boy! They slowed often so as to hear each other better, and her laughter made the surrounding travelers smile despite their own fatigue. Her heart plummeted as he described his time in capture.

"It sounds as if you were asleep most of the time you were gone. Perhaps a containment spell?"

"I have no knowledge of such things, dear Sister. I simply remember the odd-looking person who captured me, talking briefly a few times with Alara, and then I was standing in the forest. If you hadn't told me otherwise, I would think only a day had passed."

"Do you have any recollection of a Warrior woman? She was taken, too." Emmeldine studied his face intently, barely breathing.

"Nay. No one but Alara, and our encounters were brief. She asked about the baby that was born when mother died, and little else. She was so adamant that the child had lived. But she passed to the Goddess Emmeldine, did she not?"

"I used to think so — now I am not so certain. It seems many things have been hidden and kept from us most of our lives. Perhaps this is no different."

Damin gave a weary sigh and started off toward the hills their horses were approaching. After a moment, he looked back at his oldest sister with a pained expression on his face.

"If it pleases you sister, I prefer not to know any secrets. At least not yet. I do not feel ready for any such revelations. Is that acceptable to you?"

"Of course it is! I completely understand. There are things I now know that I truly wish I did not. I do not wish to burden you with such things. For now you should just focus on healing from your ordeal. New knowledge may come all too soon."

Damin did not answer. He gave a weak smile and looked away. Emmeldine decided in that moment that she would do anything in her power to convince her father to bring her brothers to the palace and live as a family. Even Ladin, who had a new mate and child. She would do whatever it took to make them feel comfortable there.

Damin now rode next to Chloe and they laughed and smiled brightly. Heart warming, she scanned the travelers and saw the remaining Crones in their wagon. Emmeldine decided to ride beside them and see if she could acquire some much-needed knowledge.

"Thank you, my dear elders, for your service today. There is no doubt your expertise in magical matters saved many lives. The whole realm is in your debt."

A Crone who had been tending to another upon the Queen's arrival at their wagon met her gaze directly, her own blue eyes bright despite her deep sagging wrinkles and stooped frame.

"I dare to speak for us all when I say the sacrifice was well worth it, my Queen. Long have we had to squelch our powers, to pretend to be less then we be. Today is the day we are finally free to be our full selves, to serve others with the power the good Goddess herself filled us with. We used our light for good." Her wrinkled face filled with tears at the last and she gently reached her hand toward the flushed, firm cheek of her ruler. The cart had stopped, and Emmeldine slowed and stopped beside it. The Crone leaned over the edge and placed a firm, dry kiss where her hand had touched the Queen. Emmeldine began to cry herself.

"Yes! I daresay I have hidden parts of myself as well. I am so sorry for you all, that you have had to hide for so long. I promise you, this shall be no more! From now on, magic will be accepted and used for good. I will find a way to make this be." Emmeldine wiped her eyes and bowed her head toward the other women in the cart, then rode off toward the edge of the convoy, suddenly desperate to be alone with her thoughts.

Later on, as they neared the palace, its tall towers standing regally in the clear blue sky, Emmeldine's heartbeat quickened and a set of warm brown eyes pierced her mind. She knew he had good reason to avoid her, but given her perilous journey she hoped he might be willing to see her, even if it would just be as friends. As the horses walked into the palace courtyard, Emmeldine, Daria, and Ramieda scanned the crowd and were greeted by loved ones with cheers and beaming smiles. Ramieda's betrothed runs up to her and they embraced tightly, faces glowing. Daria ran off to her sisters who were eagerly waving at her from the palace doors. It was apparent by the energy in the crowd and the words flying about that the entire palace was aware of at least parts of the events from the last few days. Suddenly Emmeldine found just the set of eyes she had been dreaming of, and before she knew it, she was being held firmly in Tharin's arms once again.

Chapter 41 - Then There We Are

"Your Majesty, word is spreading that there was a great battle. The people want to know who the attacker was and where they currently reside."

"Why are there no prisoners?"

"You need to choose a mate now more than ever, the realm needs to have a legitimate heir."

"There are whispers about you and Tharin — you must put them to rest by marrying the Prince."

"Why are your brothers and father moving here? This is quite unusual."

"We must advise that…"

"ENOUGH!" Emmeldine raised her voice loud enough to startle even the most stoic council member. Her cheeks flushed pink and her eyes pointed fiercely at each speaker in the room, one by one.

"I will not be questioned right now. I have just regained my brother. Good women and men were lost on the battlefield, fighting to protect us all! I am your Queen. You will have to trust me that I will give you any and all information I can as I see fit. Until such time, I suggest you keep running things as you always have. I will keep company with my family and friends while I seek healing and comfort, and I hope you do the same. Any hostility is a great change for our peaceful lands. It will take some time to come to understand it and learn how to avoid something like this from ever happening again. If you pray, then please pray for us all as we move forward with seeking peace and love."

With those final words, the flushed Queen stood up from the council chamber table, walked over to Tharin, and took his hand. His eyes sparkled merrily as he quickly jumped up and followed her out the door. The sound of gasps and some giggling caressed the backs of their ears as the doors gently closed behind them.

"You did it! I knew you could, Emmeldine. This is a day blessed by the Goddess for sure. I am so very happy!" Tharin squeezed her tightly around the waist, pushing her into his broad chest.

"I am not so sure of what I actually did, Tharin. Honestly, I may have made a large mistake. I hope this is not so. There is so much I need to tell you, much you still do not know. I think… well, if we are even going to consider being together in the future, it is time I tell you many things. Let me finish some correspondence to my father; I want him and my brothers to come here to live as soon as possible. I also need to respond to a correspondence about my baby sister. Imagine, my whole family could be reunited by the Harvest Moon! Well… not my *entire* family," she amended softly.

Emmeldine's eyes started to water, but the sudden, bold image of her sister's hateful gaze stopped the tears from falling. Tharin looked at her discerningly, then gently rubbed his thumb along the back of her palm and kissed her cheek.

"I understand — you must put family first. How about later tonight, when you are done with your queenly duties? I shall come to your chambers then." He squeezed her hand and she nodded in acceptance. With another kiss on the cheek, Tharin turned and walked back down the hall toward the workroom. Emmeldine watched him with a pleased grin as she turned back toward her own chambers, imagining her family sitting around the feast table, happy and laughing together.

After writing the letters, she sat enjoying a rare peaceful moment alone, a hot cup of seaflower tea warming as the cushy chair cradled her softly. She heard a gentle knock and Tharin quickly slipped in. She almost asked him if he was noticed, then stopped when she realized that maybe it didn't really matter. She felt a brief weight in her chest as the enormity of the coming changes in her world started to come crashing down. She looked deeply into the fluid brown eyes before her, and her body began to hum instead.

"Sit, dear Tharin — here, right beside me."

"Anything you say, Your Majesty." His eyes twinkled as he smirked playfully.

"Goodness, there is so much to tell you. I think the most important thing is about the Goddess…"

The two sat and talked softly for hours, hands clasped for much of it. Tharin was shocked, angered, confused, and ultimately resigned to her truths.

He shook his head slowly and was quiet. After a few moments he began to speak, looking at the tapestry of the Goddess behind Emmeldine, not meeting her eye, "I understand you mean no ill will, that you are trying to share with me and be truthful... even with that knowledge, I feel as if I was struck physically, sickly in my body. I need to be alone for awhile. I do hope you understand?"

She tried to search his face. To give him a tender look...yet it went unnoticed by his distant gaze. "Of course. I felt much the same way when I learned these truths. I am very sorry to have to tell you things that question, nay, disprove much of what you have always known."

With barely a whisper, he responded while turning toward the door, "How can we even know they are true? Perhaps Shaima was wrong, perhaps…"

"I *do* know, Tharin. I don't have tangible evidence, but all the events of my life now make sense. Magic is obviously a fact of nature, though we do not fully understand it. The dark figures, the Fairies, those of us that are pure Elf descendants seem to have much stronger magic than those who are multiple races. The Dwarves... " She looked at his darker features, a sinking in her stomach that made her breath catch. "Well… that is something you should think about too. Perhaps we both should think more about all of this. I am so sorry Tharin, I really am."

"Emmeldine, I need to go. Please know that I love you. I am more confused and frightened than I think I have ever been in my life, but there is a warm light in my heart where you glow. Please know that."

With a quick kiss on the cheek, Tharin departed from her chambers. She tried not to think about how everyone she loved seemed to have walked away from her in one way or another. Watching him go, a single tear trailed slowly down her cheek.

Chapter 42 - It's Never The End

Life was beginning to calm down at the palace. The council reconvened with all its members: those who knew about the recent magical events, and those who did not. With the magic users and magic supporters all in one place, they were able to explain the violent events to the entire council and be honest about what happened. Only several members resigned in outrage. Emmeldine was not surprised. Tharin spoke up during the meetings, as did one of the other male assistants that had himself witnessed the battle. She was proud of how he held his ground and defended her actions. It was decided that with so many people involved from so many areas, it was only a matter of time before the rumors would spread... and disinformation with them. To head off this possibility, the council, under Emmeldine's direction, would send emissaries to neighboring lands and royal messengers to the villages and towns. They would explain that The Queen was threatened by magical forces, and that the Queen and her Warriors persevered and fought them off. No mention would be made of the Queen using magic at that time. Nor of Alara. Unfortunately, not all matters were decided so easily. Nathalya stood to respectfully challenge the Queen.

"I beg your pardon, your Majesty, but at this time more than ever, the realm needs to see you as a strong leader, capable of carrying on your mother's legacy. There must be an heir. I hate to push you on this, but with so much being asked of people's minds and hearts, we cannot expect them to accept you mating with…"

Her pale grey eyes shot arrows at Tharin, and his dark head bowed slightly before he looked away.

"With a commoner."

Several throats were cleared as others nodded their heads.

Emmeldine felt her spine stiffen and her cheeks flush.

She made a sudden decision and tried to ignore the ice encrusting her heart as she stood to speak.

"I understand the need and... do not disagree. What do you suggest?"

There were a few murmurs and Tharin's face paled. He stood up abruptly and bolted out of the room like lightning. She felt a sting as he passed by, even though he stayed as far from her as possible, his arm literally scraping the opposite wall as he went.

"Announce your engagement to Prince Danavin immediately. His emissary has stayed behind and has agreed to this with permission of the Prince and his family. It is the only way."

"I shall." Emmeldine's face was stoic and her usually sparkling eyes were flat as she spoke listlessly. Every other body in the room was as still as a forest creature on alert.

"If it will bring peace to our lands and keep our people united, then... it must be so. I will have my scribe draw up the formal proposal immediately. We can send messengers to announce to the villages by the new moon. That is all for today." Her voice rose and punctuated the finality of what she is saying, and no one uttered a word as she looked down briefly, then forced a weak smile.

Emmeldine stood and walked briskly toward the smaller door in the room, heading to a hall Tharin was sure to not occupy. Daria rushed after her. When the door swung shut behind her, they were alone.

"Emmeldine! Stop! What are you doing?"

Emmeldine's body froze, but she did not respond.

"It is obvious that you love Tharin, and he you. Why throw that away? How many times have you told me you don't wish to be like your mother, that you wish to partner for love? You are Queen, you can do whatever you chose. Why not chose him?"

Emmeldine whipped around and narrowed her eyes, her voice audibly trembling with emotion, "Don't you think I would if I thought I could? I *want* to choose him, my body aches for his, my heart longs for his touch, his eyes… well, it is actually the eyes that are the problem. Don't you see it, Daria? He is brown-eyed and has darker features —he is of Dwarf descent. I must marry another Elf to keep the magic in the line. We cannot risk a future Queen who cannot access magic, who is not strong! With the knowledge that evil forces are out there, that Alara or her companions may attempt to take the throne again... we simply cannot risk it. No matter how much I wish I could, I cannot marry Tharin. I must bear a full Elf successor if we are to have hope of maintaining our peaceful world. Please understand," she ended in a breathless whisper.

Daria's open-mouthed expression melted into true sorrow. "Oh, my dear friend! Of course I understand. My heart cries for you, and for him. It is unfair and cruel, yet what you say makes sense. Perhaps you and Danavin will grow to share a love that is true. I do know that your father loved your mother very much. There is hope."

Daria put a hand on her friend's shoulder and forced a smile. Emmeldine tried to smile back, but her eyes were distant and her voice echoed back flatly, "Yes, there is always hope." *Hope for something different*, Emmeldine thought, as she frowned and slowly walked away.

Half a moon cycle later, Reynaldo and the princes were comfortably installed in the palace. Emmeldine continued to receive reports of Alara's containment and simple life with her father. There were several feasts to celebrate the royal family's reunification as well as the announcement that Prince Danavin had officially accepted the proposal of the Queen: he would be arriving within days for the official betrothal ceremony. The palace was once again a bright and happy home with much laughter and merriment.

The morning after one of these feasts, Emmeldine

found herself alone in her chambers. Reluctantly rising from a late night of forced merriment, she was exhausted from the restless tossing and turning caused by her tortured thoughts of Tharin and nightmares about the battle she narrowly won. A knock at the door startled her into full alertness.

"Yes? Come in, then!"

"Your Majesty, you must come quickly!" A serving lad stood in the doorway, a perplexed expression pasted on his pale face.

Emmeldine headed to the doors before the lad had finished. Her mind swirled with possibility. Was it a protest, her rogue council members turning against her? Perhaps Dono and Alara had showed up unexpectedly, or goodness forbid, a magical creature had appeared? She walked briskly down the halls, straining her ears for clues as to what was happening. She heard only the normal murmurings of palace life. The lad raced to catch up and gestured toward the front halls. She walked quicker still, disturbed by the boy's silence. She didn't waste time questioning him; she would know soon enough what she was to face. She thrust herself around the corner separating her from sight of the entryway and saw a large crowd gathered near the doorway to the outdoor courtyard. They were all standing quietly... all eyes strained in the same direction. She caught a few whispers as she passed through.

"It couldn't be?"

"...dead..."

"Surely not..."

Emmeldine's heart thundered and her muscles tightened even as she propelled them forward. As she cleared the crowded doorway, she stepped out into the morning air and it struck her like the breath of an butterfly, warm and surprisingly sweet. She scanned the courtyard and took in all the people standing stock still, staring toward the garden entryway where several women were sitting on a carved wooden bench. Emmeldine started to head in their direction and stopped cold in her path. She noticed a little girl sitting on the lap of one of the women. The girl had golden hair the exact shade as her mother's, eyes the same striking blue as Emmeldine's and Reynaldo's, and a face that was uncanny in its familiar resemblance. There was no doubt in her mind who this young girl was. Her baby sister, Cleoandra.

Emmeldine's mind split into various paths: thoughts of Alara, the impending marriage, grief over Tharin that perhaps was now unnecessary... but each tendril of thought that bubbled and tried to boil over was quickly extinguished by the sight of this lovely little girl. As Emmeldine stood there staring, the girl gracefully stood up and looked straight at her big sister. The feelings in the young Queen's heart upon locking eyes with this tiny person began to fill up and spread like a warmth of hope, of promise, of a future full of love. It felt like magic.

Epilogue – New Beginnings

Emmeldine realized she was gripping Cleoandra's hand rather tightly and lightened her grasp. They were walking through the north garden, much as the elder sister often had with their mother. Emmeldine teared up at the thought of her baby sister never knowing her own mother. Then again, Emmeldine found herself teary quite frequently these days. Cleo looked up at her with bright blue eyes and Emmeldine smiled gently. She reminded herself that her sister was used to being referred to as Bessine, the name her caregivers had given her after their Aunt Claraceit had passed to the great beyond. At least *that* part of the whole charade had been true.

Emmeldine had pieced together the story over the last few moons and had come to understand that Claraceit had been trying to save her baby sister from a life of hardship and possibly rejection. Cleo had been born with abnormalities, possibly due to their mothers mature age at conception. Regardless of why, children born with differences were normally looked down upon, and a royal birth could prove especially problematic once word got out that the heir in waiting was not well. Thus, Claraceit had personally cared for the infant her first year and found Healers who were able to help her. Emmeldine suspected the work of a Witch, but no one would confirm this. In any case, the result was the beautiful, healthy little girl before her. Tears welled up again as Emmeldine thought of her sister losing a second mother at only one pass of the seasons. Claraceit's ladies cared for her as their own and kept her hidden until such time that the young girl could decide for herself to re-enter her royal family. Which she had.

Cleo squinted up with wide blue eyes. "Tell me more, please? About our mother?"

Emmeldine felt a tight grip on her heart, a slow tearing that felt never ending, yet somehow mending at the same time. She took a deep breath and smiled down at the fair-headed little princess.

"Let's see. You should know, Cleo...Er... Bessine, that mother wanted you ever so badly. She had been trying for a while to conceive and you were her blessing. She glowed with love and pride to have you inside her."

Cleo's smile took up her entire delicate face, her cheeks looking as if they may burst. "It's ok Emmeldine, if you wish to call me Cleo, or Cleoandra. I like it. I like having a name chosen by my kin. By the Queen, at that!" She laughed and it sounded like pure joy.

"Really? Can I call you Cleo? I don't want to force you to make a change you are uncomfortable with. I know the last season has been trying for you and full of change. To change your name also... well, that's a big thing for a little girl."

"Perhaps just you call me Cleo for now? Then I shall see how I feel about it. Would that be alright?"

"Of course! I am honored, dear sister. Cleo. Thank you." Emmeldine wiped away a tear from her cheek and reached for her sister's small hand.

They walked further into the garden, swinging their arms playfully.

"Might I ask something of you?" The young girl spoke softly, eyes fixed upon the soft brown earth which they tread.

"Anything. You need only open your mouth and I shall use all my queenly powers to fulfill your wish!" Emmeldine's lips turned up and her eyes sparkled until she noticed the serious expression on her little sister's face. She stopped walking and turned to face her, her own expression now serious as well. "What is it Cleo? It's ok, you can speak freely with me." She gently squeezed Cleo's hand and took a step back to better read her face.

"I... well, I would like to know more about our sister, Alara. I have been warned not to speak with you about her, yet I long to know of her. Is this allowed?" Cleo continued to study her feet while she spoke but looked up briefly with watery eyes.

"Oh, dear sister! Of course. It is expected you will be curious and longing and … I understand. It is hard for me to speak of our sister Alara, this is true. Yet you do indeed deserve to know of her. I cannot tell you certain things till you are older, but let me think a moment of what you should know now." Emmeldine stared off into a bed of tall white moon drops, and then with a sigh, she forced a small smile and began.

"Alara was always brave. She loved horses; I don't know if she still does. We… we haven't spoken much of late. Alara was adventurous and would explore anywhere she could find. She was very loving when she was young — she never seemed to be able to get enough attention. She craved… well, I'm not exactly sure what she craved, but it did not seem we were able to give it to her…" she trailed off, then shook her head. "I'm sorry. This must be confusing to a little girl — I wish I had more to tell you." Emmeldine looked up with moist blue eyes sparkling and stared into the fluffy clouds overhead, her frown deepening as she noticed their darkening color. She reached out to hold her sister's small warm hand again. "Come, Cleo, let us get inside and have some tea. I sense a storm brewing."

"Yes, sister. Since you may call me Cleo, might I call you Emmy? When we are alone? I know I am to refer to you as my sister Queen when at court. My minders taught me."

Emmeldine's stoic face broke into a wide smile as she gently squeezed Cleo's hand. "Oh yes! I think that best, dear sister! I am glad to hear your minders raised you so well, and gladder still you want familiarity with me. Please, continue to ask me anything. I shall do my best to respond as openly and honestly as I may. Sometimes being grown means you have to keep things to yourself. I hope you can forgive me this?"

Cleo's eyes narrowed and her lips tightened, but then she shrugged her shoulders and forced a small smile. "I'm not certain I do understand, Emmy, but I shall do my best. Can we have some of those tiny red cakes with tea?"

"Absolutely! I shall order a huge tray for us! After all, what is the privilege of being rulers if we cannot indulge in a special treat now and again?" She laughed and they walked quickly back towards the palace, arms swinging gaily once again. Dark clouds followed swiftly behind, covering the land in shadows as they entered the sparkling marble hall, oblivious to the rain and wind that started swirling behind them.

Author's Note

This story was born out of my love of fantasy and writing. The people and events in this story flowed out of me in a way that did indeed feel magical. The story is not complete. There is much more to explore in the land of Trimeria and Emmeldine's story is not done. Please follow the link below to see an exclusive sneak peek into the upcoming sequel, "Something Further."

tinyurl.com/y8cyxllk

About the Author

Corrine Taiji is a school counselor by day and a super mama to two spunky boys by night. During the early years of parenting, Corrine was looking for something outside of motherhood to feed her spirit and took some creative writing classes. During one of these courses, the beginning of Something Different was born. When not mothering or writing, Corrine enjoys hiking, reading, socializing and spending time with her husband Garrett.

Also By The Author

E-Love: A true tale of the online dating world and what it took to find The One.

Available on Amazon : tinyurl.com/y8po5l8o

Coming Soon

Something Further: Book 2 in the Something Trilogy

For a sneak preview please go here: tinyurl.com/y8cyxllk